ABOUT THIS BOOK

Holiday romance, second chances, and new beginnings... *The Manger House* is a heartwarming, romantic women's fiction about the true meaning of Christmas.

Tatum Sageberry always wanted to open an animal shelter. Now she's got the property but not a clue where to begin.

Enter local bachelor Rip Van Dam, a family friend who's been looking for a chance to spend time with the pretty new islander. What's more? He's a pet-lover, too. But Tatum has only one thing on her mind, and it has nothing to do with meeting under the mistletoe.

Meanwhile, Tatum's sisters are in the thick of their own fresh starts. Cadence is opening her own business: an all-inclusive events venue. And just in time for the holiday season. But with property management, the new business, and her return to the classroom—it's too much, and she's about to lose her grip for good.

Darla's life has been turned upside down, and she is second-guessing *everything*, not the least of which is the only anchor she has: teaching. Work was always a safe haven for the sensible thirtysomething, but now a new romance is drifting in like softly falling snow, her sisters are starting new businesses, and Darla is going through the biggest change of her life. If things don't settle down fast, Darla can't imagine sticking around Heirloom Island for much longer.

This Christmas could be the best ever—complete with the sisters' famous gooseberry pie, decked halls, and hot cocoa by the fire. But only if they can find their holiday spirit *together*, amid all the madness of the yuletide season.

Head to Heirloom Island in this heartwarming series about three sisters and the charming small town they've come to call home. With enemies-to-lovers romance, sister drama, and small-town charm, The Manger House *is the perfect Christmas story.*

the manger house

an heirloom island novel

ELIZABETH BROMKE

This book is a work of fiction. Names, characters, places, and events are products of the author's imagination. Any resemblance to locations, events, or people (living or dead) is purely coincidental.

Copyright © 2021 Elizabeth Bromke

All rights reserved.

Cover design by Red Leaf Cover Design

The reproduction or distribution of this book without permission is a theft. If you would like to share this book or any part thereof (reviews excepted), please contact us through our website:

elizabethbromke.com

THE MANGER HOUSE

Publishing in the Pines

White Mountains, Arizona

You can read these books in order for extra enjoyment.

Book 1: The Boardwalk House

Book 2: The Manger House

Book 3: The Abbey House

CHAPTER 1—TATUM

Tatum Sageberry sat in her little red truck at the bottom of a snowy drive. Pine trees flecked either side of the white path that wound its way faintly from where her engine idled all the way up fifty yards to a farmhouse, red to match her truck. Tatum considered the coincidence in color to be a good omen.

Asleep on the back seat were her dogs, Angus, Marley, and Serena, huddled in a furry heap atop a woven wool blanket. Back home, in the house on the boardwalk, awaited her cat, Charm.

The windshield wipers swept like a pair of squeaky pendulums, clearing away a slowly building layer of flurries. Tatum rested her chin on the steering wheel and stared with wonder.

"Good things come to those who rush in," she murmured to herself, only mildly aware that she'd butchered two expressions and spliced them into one untruth. She glanced in the rearview at her snoring children. They deserved this, those pups. Even Charm, that obnoxious pill of a feline, deserved this. They deserved room to roam and a snowy woodland to get lost in. A big house with lots of rugs and a fireplace and a mudroom just for them.

Yes. Her pets deserved this.

But did Tatum?

What had she done in life? Not much. Still, she'd managed to get herself, her sister, and her animals here to Heirloom Island in one piece. Give or take. She'd managed to find a property for sale, then beg, borrow, and steal her way into purchasing it. And here she was, with her own set of keys, on Thanksgiving Eve, ready to do a private walk-through. Size everything up without the influence of Darla and Cadence, who meant well, but who seemed to see the bad in everything.

"Well. What are we waiting for?" Tatum asked the motley crew in back.

Tails started thumping, tongues wagging. The furbabies were awake.

Tatum couldn't help it. She let a silly grin take

over her face as she rolled her finger around the radio dial until "Jingle Bells" spilled out of the speakers. Everything was perfect. The setting. The company. And even the song. The truck tires crunched over freshly fallen snow, and Tatum daydreamed about turning the farm into her dream: Heirloom Island's own animal rescue. And maybe, one day, a place that would rescue Tatum, too. Not from abuse or homelessness, but from a life of moorlessness. A life of nothing.

CHAPTER 2—CADENCE

Cadence Van Dam closed the teacher edition math textbook just as her last student left the classroom. She checked her watch, an anniversary gift from Hendrik and one of many special treasures he'd left her. It was the day before Thanksgiving, and the afternoon could not be crazier. At four, Darla had a scan at the OBGYN in Birch Harbor, and Cadence would drive her. After that, they really needed to shop for last-minute essentials for the next day. Before bed, Cadence planned to undertake a full house-cleaning, with Mila's help. Then, she needed to frame out how she was going to make her proposition the next day.

Sure, over the past few months, things had been going well enough. With her sisters renting the house next door and paying a fair amount, Cadence was more than making ends meet, which was nice. But since Lotte and Fay had moved, and since Mila was *planning* to move, Cadence had begun to wonder if the housing arrangements *really* made sense. Especially with Darla's due date right around the corner.

Wouldn't it be better if the three sisters all roomed? Then Darla would have help, and Tatum would have their good influences, and Cadence... well, Cadence would have *company*.

In fact, Mila's impending move had caused her a fresh wave of anxiety, a distraction just in time for Darla's big excitement to take place. Cadence was very likely even more excited than Darla for the baby's arrival. She hadn't admitted this, but it was probably evident in her shopping habits—she handled all the selecting and purchasing of baby basics—and in her nonstop baby chat. Why didn't Darla want to learn the child's sex? What first names did she have in mind? Would she give the little one Hunter's surname—*no*, thank goodness—or the Sageberry family name?

But Darla, despite her big talk about bucket lists and baby fever and dreams come true, had changed in her pregnancy. Maybe it was the fact that she was in a new town, or maybe it was the fact that she'd be starting a family without a partner. Cadence had not, however, stopped to consider that Darla's turn inward could be a direct result of Cadence's badgering. She hadn't considered this because Cadence needed this baby. She needed this baby—and the presence of her sisters—in order to fill the void that for a year now had been growing to the size of a black hole. The void that Hendrik had left in his wake. The one that one year of grieving did nothing to diminish, especially as they came up on the holidays.

She closed and locked her classroom door and started down the hall toward the family room, where Darla held her last class of the day: Dramatic Literature. It was the only way she could figure to teach language arts to the adolescent set—through the use of the works she'd produced when she was a stage manager in the Wayne State theater program—but it worked. Especially now, as "O Holy Night" reverberated down the hall and Cadence remembered that the holiday season was just too much for the poor kids to languish in *Hamlet*. Darla had seamlessly—and with the full support of the headmaster and Father Richard—transitioned into using most of her students to put up the Nativity play that Christmas.

Come spring, it'd be Simon Peter. She was all in—even despite her impending life change. And this worried Cadence. It worried her to the bone. It worried her so much that she had begun to wonder what her role would *really* become now that Darla and the baby and Tatum and her animals were under her charge. Cadence had begun to wonder, in fact, if she might have made the wrong choice in trying to start her new business and rejoining St. Mary's.

Maybe she was meant to do the thing that she knew how to do best: put others first. Maybe putting herself first, for once, was the wrong play. Maybe pushing ahead and forging her own path had been the wrong decision all along—back when she first moved to the island and took a risk on loving an older man. And again now, as she tried to overhaul her life and create the financial freedom she'd so enjoyed in her marriage.

Maybe Cadence was doing it all wrong.

CHAPTER 3—DARLA

Darla cupped one hand beneath her protruding belly and pointed the other downstage. "Okay, we've got five minutes. Let's run through Joseph's and Mary's lines at the manger."

The eighth-grade pair, giddy with the idea that they were a *couple*—even though Mary was a virgin—stood awkwardly next to each other. Mary collected the prop Baby Jesus, complete in his swaddling gown, from the wooden bed and cradled him in her arms.

"Too brusque!" Darla called.

"What does *brusque* mean?" the girl called back. The enthusiasm for the play wasn't quite *there* yet, and they had exactly three weeks to go before dress rehearsals.

"Mary"—Darla believed in using their character names even if they were only blocking it out—"you've just given birth to the Savior. You're a young girl. You're scared. You're staying in a *barn*, but you're a mother now." Darla moved closer to downstage center. "Yes, you might be uncomfortable. Yes, you're probably in pain and confused, but you're not going to be *rough* with God's Only Son."

The girl studied the plastic doll. "Maybe we need a real baby, then."

Darla didn't disagree, but her due date fell on the week of dress rehearsals, and the plan was to have the baby, take a week off, and return to school in time for opening night. She'd need one of her sisters to step in and oversee things—the appointed assistant director and stage manager were hanger-on seventh graders without vision, after all. But, it could be done. As long as due dates could be trusted.

As a new mother, all Darla had to go on was trust: trust in the nine-month incubation period, trust in her sisters to help, and trust in herself to manage it all. And if Darla couldn't manage it all, then what? Would she crawl back to Detroit and beg Hunter to give her another chance? Of course not. Darla had only one option: to make this work. Yes. She'd continue teaching, she'd raise her baby, she'd nurture her rekindled bond with Cadence and help Tatum with her own fledgling bucket-list dream.

She'd do it all. *Somehow*.

"Ready?" Cadence's voice interrupted the set, and Darla swiveled to wave her sister off.

"I just need five minutes."

"Ms. Sageberry, you said that five minutes ago," Joseph complained.

Darla gave him a pointed look. "We could have been done five minutes ago if you'd get your blocking right. One more time, you two. Exit and reenter. Mary," Darla directed the girl, "this time, pretend the doll is the real thing."

As the two kids trudged up and behind the curtain, then walked back through the scene, Cadence joined Darla at what was supposed to be the apron of the stage, but what was actually just the tape she'd put down to indicate such. "Are you going to cast the baby as Jesus?"

"What baby?" Darla asked distractedly.

Cadence scoffed. "*Your* baby."

"Timing'll be all wrong. If I had him or her, like, *today*, maybe. That would put us at nearly four weeks, and I think it could work. But according to my due date—"

"I was joking. And anyway, according to your due date," Cadence cut in, "you should be on bedrest by now. Not on your feet directing a play. Wrap it up, and let's go. We're going to miss the ferry."

"The ferry?" Darla dismissed her students, reminding them quickly that rehearsals resumed Monday after school. She packed her school tote and followed Cadence, who walked with purpose down the hall and toward the teacher parking lot. "I thought we were taking the boat?"

Earlier that year, Mason Acton had connected Cadence with a good boat mechanic on the island. Turned out Hendrik had used the guy before, but there wasn't any familiarity or friendliness between them, and Cadence, apparently, had just as soon lost the man's phone number. She reported that by the time she looked for it again, winter was descending on Heirloom Island, and Cadence had figured there wouldn't be much boating. She hadn't thought about all of Darla's appointments.

And she certainly hadn't thought of getting her sister to the mainland on the *big day*.

But now her boat was acting up again, and for

today, at least, they'd have to take the ferry. Darla hated this, but what choice did they have?

"Sorry, I thought you knew. The boat won't start."

Darla groaned. They made it to Cadence's car, the frigid air sweeping them inside where Cadence started the engine and blasted the heat.

"We need to get it fixed," Darla pointed out on their way to the ferry. "Or we need to get a new boat."

"A new boat is a big expense." But surely Cadence agreed that the boat needed fixing. Darla wondered if the real reason she hadn't fixed it had less to do with money and more to do with hard feelings. It'd be uncomfortable to drive one's deceased husband's craft. After all, it was named for his previous wife, Katarina. One would have thought Hendrik would have renamed a boat.

Tentatively, Darla asked about this. "Could you rename her? The boat, I mean?"

Cadence threw her a sharp look. "Renaming a boat is bad luck."

Surely, though, people rename boats, Darla thought. In fact, she was fairly positive that you *could* rename a boat if you did it right—by removing all traces of the original name. She said to her sister, "All you'd have to do is paint on a new name, right? The *real* Katarina has passed anyway."

Cadence didn't reply to that, and Darla figured it was too long of a shot to suggest she just sell the *Katarina* and buy a new one and name it *Cadence*. Something maybe Hendrik ought to have done.

It was almost as if, Darla wondered for her sister, Hendrik had never actually moved on. As if Katarina weren't dead. At least, not *really*.

CHAPTER 4—TATUM

Tatum had spent the night at the farm, which was a silly thing to have done. She hadn't been prepared—not enough blankets, no pillows. Only her dogs for warmth. But once she'd gotten there, she'd been seized by a need to test things out.

Of course, Tatum wasn't going to live on the farm. The entirety of the property would be dedicated to the shelter and outbuildings-turned-dog-runs. Even so, how could Tatum know if the animals would be safe there overnight if she herself wasn't comfortable with it?

So, she'd slept on the spare wool blankets she kept for the dogs in the back seat of the truck. They'd cuddled together and waited for the sun to bleed down past the little kitchen window. This was part of what had called Tatum to the place: that it had been a house first. A home, actually. Somebody's home, and definitely even somebody with dogs and cats and horses and goats and cows and chickens of their own. From all that Tatum had read about her new place on Pine Beach Way, it had been a working farm. A *real* working farm, complete with cows for milking, sheep for shearing, and horses for riding—and even some light gardens at the far inland edge. That was another thing Tatum loved about Pine Beach Farm—how it could be a place of sustainable living. Everything Tatum would ever—could ever—need, she could have right there, on her very own farm and in her very own little animal house. She could grow vegetables and maybe, one day, bring over an alpaca or something exotic from which she'd shave fleece—did alpacas have fleece, or what was it called?

Anyway, it was just as well that Tatum spent the evening away from home. Cadence and Darla had taken the ferry into town for another prenatal appointment and wanted to do a little shopping after. Tatum, not one to enjoy errands, had readily agreed to get up bright and early Thanksgiving morning to clean and cook and get all ready for their guests. Their mother, Pat, and the girls—Lotte, Fay, and Mila.

So, here she was. Back at her sister's boardwalk house, bright and early, with her clan of canines in tow. "Hello-oo?" Tatum bellowed into the whitewashed abyss once the dogs and Charm the cat had been fed and settled. "I don't smell any coffee!"

Cadence appeared from the kitchen, her face twisted up to match her messy French do. "Where *were* you?"

"At the farm." Tatum turned defensive on a dime. "I told you—*why*? What's wrong?"

"We were trying to call you. Text you—*find* you."

"You could have driven to the farm—"

"Tatum," Cadence hissed, her eyes flying upstairs. "It's Darla. She had her OB appointment last night. *Remember?*"

Of course Tatum *remembered*. But, so what? Darla had at least two or three weeks until her due date. She was working her life away at school. Everything was fine.

Right?

Panic streaked like a bolt of lightning across Tatum's heart as she realized that maybe everything was not fine. And if Cadence's hushed hisses and pained looks were any indication, things were absolutely *not* fine. Not even close.

"What." The word fell out of Tatum's mouth like an anchor.

Cadence drew closer, her eyes again flicking upstairs. It was then that Tatum realized how empty the house had seemed when she'd gone over to situate the pets. How hungry Charm was. How needy. As if no one had been home last night.

"Cadence, *what* is it?"

"Darla's not having…just…*a baby*."

"Well, what in the world is she having?" Pictures of newborn polar bear cubs and caribou calves with white downy fur played across Tatum's brain like a snowy movie reel. Laughter crept into the back of her throat at the thought of Darla having an animal baby, and she knew she was being immature and ridiculous, but she couldn't help it. She was about to have the giggles. Until Cadence, whose face remained stony, replied.

"Twins."

CHAPTER 5—CADENCE

Cadence dropped the news on Tatum with as much gravitas as she could muster since she had a feeling Tatum wouldn't immediately appreciate how serious a situation they were in.

Or how *exciting*.

Tatum was appropriately shocked. "How could that be? She's been going to the doctor regularly."

"That doesn't ward off twins, you know." Cadence ushered her little sister into the kitchen. It was important that Darla use the morning to rest, after all.

Tatum glared. "You know what I mean. How did the doctors not *see* this before? Didn't she have an ultrasound already?"

"Yes, but that was early on—very early—and little babies are, well, *little*." A smile pooled across Cadence's mouth. For her, news of twins was nothing short of thrilling. *Twins!* A new wave of excitement coursed through Cadence's body. Their lives had already changed so much in a matter of months, and they'd expected this new, other huge change. But twins? It was double the transformation in the Sageberrys' lives. Twins meant two cribs. Two car seats. A double stroller. A bigger room? Mentally, Cadence pictured Darla's bedroom next door. She'd gotten the master suite in order to accommodate the bassinet and all baby bath products. But now she'd need two bassinets. Or what if Darla didn't want to use bassinets at all? Wasn't co-sleeping *in*? Wasn't co-sleeping *dangerous*? Cadence worried her lip when she realized Tatum was staring at her, waiting for a further explanation.

"Wouldn't something else suggest twins? Like a special test or something? And also, aren't most twins born, like, a month or two early, even?" Tatum scavenged the pantry for a muffin, then grabbed a mug for coffee, handily splashing the lukewarm dregs from earlier into the mug. Bright and early had been their plan, originally, but to Cadence that meant six o'clock. To Tatum, it meant nine or so. Of course, the plan had been crafted before Cadence and Darla had the OB appointment. Before the bombshell news.

"Two months would be dramatic, but yes. You're right," Cadence acknowledged. "Usually, people know. With Darla, though, they didn't. As for her due date—that's irrelevant now. Her age coupled with the fact that we didn't know there were two babies makes her a bit of a high risk, so they're going to induce."

"You mean she'll deliver early." Tatum's confusion turned to glee, and this was where Cadence and Tatum's sisterhood shone: in their shared happiness for Darla and the future. The promise of a new generation.

Cadence waited for Tatum to lower her coffee before responding. "Yes. Actually, the doctors were pretty adamant that we expedite the whole thing. They wanted to schedule her immediately."

"Immediately? Like, Monday morning, or—?"

"Like today."

Tatum shuffled backward, her arms waving in front of her as if to ward off her own disbelief. "It's Thanksgiving."

"Unborn babies don't really care about Thanksgiving, Tate."

"But doctors do! What doctor wants to give up the tastiest holiday of the year?" Tatum reddened. "I mean—if they think Darla needs to deliver, I support that. It's just...crazy, right?"

Cadence smiled and shook her head, swiping Tatum's crumbs into her palm and brushing them into the trash before carrying her coffee mug to the sink. "To answer your question, *good* doctors are willing to give up turkey in order to help their patients. They do this all the time—sacrifice special occasions for their career." Her head snapped up. "A lot of people sacrifice things for their careers, you know."

"True," Tatum agreed airily. "Even their families."

The two shared a look, and a dozen things could have passed between them. The reminder of losing their dad too young, before he'd even retired. The reminder that they'd grown up as latchkey kids while both parents worked hard at often-unforgiving jobs and sometimes more than one a piece. Not only that, though. Cadence, too, felt Tatum's quiet acknowledgment of the route that Cadence herself had taken—the road less traveled in the context of the Sageberrys' upbringing. Marrying Hendrik was like leaving the world she knew for one that only existed in storybooks. One in which there never seemed to be a conflict with attending the girls' school plays or spelling bees because there wasn't a career. Van Dam money had covered everything. Until the bitter end.

Then again, there was one conflict that split across their lives like two tectonic plates breaking apart and forcing an earthquake from below. The unlikely reality that two people in the same family could come down with fatal illnesses within the same timeframe. *Die* within the same timeframe. That conflict wasn't a career versus family thing, though. There was no sacrificing work to tend to her ill husband, and of course there was no sacrificing her husband to tend to work. Cadence had quit teaching when they'd married. In the end, though, there was a sacrifice to be made. The sacrifice of saying goodbye to her father in order to say goodbye to her husband.

Cadence forced a bright smile across her face. Darla and Tatum had returned to her life, and she knew what a precious gift she'd been given. A second chance to keep her family close. She would give up anything to keep them, too. Anything in the world. Even the life she'd carved for herself on the boardwalk. Content in her resolve, she gave the countertop a final wipe with a paper towel and said, "Luckily, we put each other first. And anyway, none of us has to make that sort of sacrifice. Family first. Right?"

But Tatum was on her phone, studying something with a feverish expression.

"What is it?"

Tatum turned the phone screen to show Cadence what had captured her attention so totally. There, beneath the cracked-like-an-egg screen protector, was a social media page. Cadence read aloud from the page name. "Heirloom Island Community for Our Pets." Her eyes fell to the subheading. "Three hundred members, wow. I didn't realize islanders were active on that site."

"It's not the page." Tatum thrust the phone closer. "Look at the post."

Cadence read an all-capital-letters announcement, complete with a garland of asterisks and sad-face emojis.

***HELP!!! THIS SWEET CAT AND HER LITTER OF SEVEN JUST FOUND IN BACK OF THE BAIT SHOP DESPERATELY NEED FULL-TIME FOSTER CARE THROUGH THE HOLIDAY WEEKEND. ALL ISLAND

FOSTERS ARE FULL. PLEASE SHARE FAR AND WIDE AND HELP US GET THIS PRECIOUS FELINE FAMILY A HOME SO THEY DON'T FREEZE TO DEATH OUT THERE!!!***

"Tate," Cadence started. Tatum pulled the phone back as her frown turned deep. "That's so sad." The statement was meant as a blow-off, and not because Cadence wasn't genuinely sad for the cat and her kittens, but because they had to leave in less than thirty minutes. Darla needed to be up and dressed and packed, and the three of them needed to get to the hospital in Lakeview. They had a Thanksgiving dinner to cancel, and they had twins to welcome into the world. That very day. An edginess crept beneath Cadence's skin. "I'm sure someone will take them. Social media is so powerful these days. They'll get a home in no time. Check back later tonight. Mark my words, they'll be settled in some little old lady's mudroom with a space heater and a bowl of milk."

Tatum shook her head, though. She looked at Cadence pleadingly. "Cadence, this is it."

"Tate, today is the day our sister is giving birth. *Tatum*, Darla is going into *surgery*, possibly. If she doesn't dilate with the induction, they will perform a C-section. It's…serious."

"I know," Tatum replied, her reverie breaking only to wash back over her countenance. "It's just—the comments say that they found the cats three days ago. The Bait Shop owner won't keep them. They need a place, and I can help. This could be my first rescue."

"Why don't you send them a message and explain that you're away today but you can check in tomorrow?" Cadence was being reasonable, she thought. Very reasonable and compassionate to all parties concerned, not the least of whom was Darla, the pregnant one.

Before Tatum could reply, Darla appeared in the doorway, her hand on her protruding belly, her face clean and dark hair neat. She wore the soft cotton pajama set they'd bought before returning home last night. She looked ready to leave. "Is everything okay?" Darla asked, her face crinkling in worry.

"Well," Tatum began, to Cadence's incredulity, "what time are you supposed to check into the hospital, exactly?"

Cadence threw her another sharper look, and Tatum held up her hands in surrender. "I'm just…*asking*."

CHAPTER 6—DARLA

"I check into the hospital this morning. Why? What's wrong?" Darla pressed Tatum. "Do you have to be somewhere?"

"Everything is *fine*," Cadence said, giving Tatum a sharp look. "Tatum was going to take in a litter of stray kittens, but she wasn't thinking about our big news."

"*Our* big news?" Darla couldn't help the little dig. Cadence's overprotectiveness had grown into a monster. She turned again to Tatum. "The litter—you're going to take them in?" She knew what this meant to her sister despite the big drama of the day. Darla's hand moved in wide circles around her belly. She felt Cadence's stare on her and looked up at her older sister, whose brown hair was swept back in a pretty braid. Her makeup impeccable, and her outfit at once comfortable and chic, she could have been the mother of the bride. Or the mother of the mother-to-be, as the case was.

"No," Tatum said. "I'm going to try and get them tomorrow." Her voice deflated and her shoulders drooping, she reminded Darla of when they were teenagers and Tatum had been forced to join the family for church even though there'd been a hurt baby bird panting beneath the dogwood tree in their front yard. Tatum had never been one for church anyway, and with a wounded animal to tend to, it'd seemed the more saintly thing to do was to help the animal. Wouldn't God have preferred that? Their parents had convinced Tatum to move the little winged thing into an old shoebox for safe keeping until they'd returned from Mass.

Darla considered this. She knew Tatum's situation, and she knew it could be weeks before everything was set up and running. Tatum wasn't quite ready to take on any rescues, but she was excited. So excited, in fact, that she'd camped out in the farmhouse across the island in order to get a feel for it. Perhaps that was why they couldn't get in touch with Tatum all night, but it hadn't bothered Darla as much as it had Cadence. Now, of course, Darla wanted Tatum at the birth, but did she really need to be there all morning during the prep? Couldn't they call her when things were heating up? It might be hours until anything substantial happened at the hospital. Anyway, even their mother wasn't leaving Detroit for another hour, and she had a drive ahead of her.

"Tate," Darla said, "why don't you go ahead and pick them up? Get them situated—the kittens, I mean. We'll be at the hospital, and we aren't going anywhere." Cadence didn't laugh, but Tatum's face lit up. Darla went on. "We'll call you when it's getting closer to go-time. Right, Cade?"

Cadence pursed her lips but tilted her head at Tatum. "Are you going to keep your phone on you?"

"I promise. I *swear*." Tatum hopped up and down before grabbing Darla's hands from her belly and squeezing them. "I love you. Call me as soon as you need me—I'll literally sprint there. I'll swim if I have to."

"You might have to. We're taking the boat, and it's Thanksgiving," Darla replied, stealing a look at Cadence. "We *are* taking the boat. Right?"

Cadence leaned closer to the window to look out at the water. Darla knew what she was worried about, of course. She was worried about whether the boat would be fixed in time. Darla wasn't, though.

She had managed to find the phone number for the boat mechanic Hendrik used to use. A guy by the name of Jimmy Winters. He was a loner, or at least that's what Darla took him to be: an islander whose yellow pages business entry was one line, no frills: *Jimmy Winters, Marine Mechanic*, followed by what must have been his landline number; because the first time Darla had called, she'd gotten what sounded distinctly like an old-fashioned answering machine, complete with a beep. Darla had left a message, apologizing profusely for calling on the holiday and promising to pay double his usual rate. He'd called back not five minutes later, apologizing that he hadn't answered. He hadn't had any plans for the day, anyway, and he was happy to help Cadence, whom he recalled from way back when.

Now, he toiled away at the boat, and signs of life were emerging through sputtering engine noises here and there.

"I hope," Cadence replied to Darla. "If the boat doesn't get fixed, then we'll call Mason."

Darla stiffened at his name. Mason would be a last resort. It was too awkward for her to see him, especially in her present condition.

"I'm sure everything will work out," Cadence added, apparently aware of the effect her suggestion had on Darla. "Jimmy will fix our boat. Tatum'll catch the ferry. We'll meet at the hospital when it looks like the babies are close."

"And after the delivery, Tatum can order in a big stuffed turkey with all the fixings."

"Oh, don't worry about that." Cadence tsked with her finger. "I've already told the girls that we'll delay Thanksgiving dinner. We'll have it here. Just a little later than planned."

"I might not be home for a few days," Darla pointed out. "And that's if all goes well."

"Sis, you might not be home for a week or more, depending. Labor is no joke, and delivering *twins* is double the drama."

"Oh, no." Darla brushed her sister off. "In a week, I plan to be running rehearsals for the Christmas show."

Neither sister answered.

Darla bristled at their silence and the glance they exchanged. "What?"

Cadence offered a tight smile. Tatum shrugged.

But Darla knew she was right. That she'd be one of *those* moms. The ones with a flat stomach just weeks after childbirth. The ones who master sleep routines and feeding cycles. Who return to work and pump in the break room, filling up bags of breast milk like dairy cows for the gurgling happy baby back at home, waiting to spend a quiet, peaceful evening with Mom.

They'd see. Darla would have these babies, take a week—ten days tops—to recover, then hit the ground running. She could do it all.

And she would.

CHAPTER 7—TATUM

Tatum wasted no time in reaching out to the social media poster, then driving directly to the Bait Shop. She figured she could get the phone call to report to the hospital at any moment, and so she'd have to get the cat and her kittens fast, pull together supplies, then get everything to the farm within an hour or so. She hoped to have a chance to settle them before rushing back to the ferry and praying that she could get to the mainland that way.

"Hi," she said to the shopkeeper, a familiar face. "Are you the one who posted about the cat and her kittens?"

"Yes, I'm Sharon," the portly, plain-looking woman replied easily. "Come on back here." As they walked through the cramped shop and toward a back storeroom, the woman explained the circumstances surrounding the feline family. Her midwestern Michigander dialect was stronger than Tatum was used to. A fine example of a true island local, this kind woman. "Just a coupla days ago I took the trash out, and I heard a little mew, and I lifted up a big, ol' piece of cardboard, ya see, and there she was, mama and her babies." They arrived at a far corner of the storeroom, behind a tower of boxes. Within the fortress was the mother cat in question, with her kittens, snuggled in a box. The mother was white as newly fallen snow, and half of her kittens were, too. The other half were a motley calico mix.

Tatum dropped to her knees and reached for the furballs as Sharon went on. "Anywho, my folks own this place, and they're older. They live out in the house in back of the shop. I'd take this bunch home if I could, but my husband'd have a hissy fit, so I can't. My folks aren't keen on us having a litter of cats back here on account'a the county health department. Now, they never do make a visit to the island 'cept for health inspections, but it's not worth the hassle. Just in case, y'know."

"Right." Tatum had tuned her out and was instead visualizing herself with the kittens. Were there no mother, Tatum might have had to bottle-feed them. She wondered if she could simply take them back to the boardwalk house for the time being, but that wouldn't do. New mother cats were nervous, and with four dogs and another cat in the house and no safeguard against barking, the boardwalk house would be too stressful. No, Tatum needed to create a safe, secure place where the mama and babies would be comfortable and warm and able to thrive.

And, as she'd already considered, this could be her chance to really get rolling.

"I'll take them. I'm opening a shelter on the south side of the island up from the shore. It's the old Andersen farm. Maybe you knew them?" Tatum looked up at Sharon.

"Sure I did. Dated an Andersen in high school, in fact. Didn't go anywhere, of course." She belted out a laugh. "But he was a fiddle, that one. Fit, I mean." She grabbed a handful of her stomach. "Unlike me. I'm a curvy gal, and you'd be hard-pressed to find a man with a taste for curves, even on Heirloom. They see those lithe tourists hop out of speedboats and just drool, I tell ya, Tatum."

Tatum stood and smoothed her hands down her jeans. "Sharon," she said, "thank you."

"Me? Thank me for what?" Sharon's heavy brows shot up her forehead and disappeared into a thatch of mousey-brown bangs.

"For posting about these sweet little things," Tatum replied. "A lot of people would just ignore them. Maybe feed them for a while until the mother wanders off and the babies are left." Tatum looked at Sharon with admiration. "You cared enough."

Sharon seemed unfazed by the compliment. She huffed and replied, "You're opening a what? An animal shelter?"

"That's right," Tatum answered, beaming. "Heirloom Island's first animal shelter."

WITH THE MOTHER cat stowed in Charm's old travel kennel and the kittens still in their box from the Bait Shop, Tatum made her way out to the farm. The mama mewed loudly the whole drive. Unaccustomed to riding in cars, but also scared to be separated from her young, Tatum knew.

The first order of business, once they arrived, was building a fire in the woodstove and settling the cat family as well as she could. She didn't yet have all the supplies she needed, but she could make do.

At the farm, Tatum got to work, locking into place one of her extra-large wire dog kennels and lining it with an old quilt she'd gotten from a thrift store inland. Assuming the kittens might still prefer the coziness of close quarters, she added a small dog bed that had once belonged to Serena. Once everything in the kennel was set and the fire was underway, Tatum carefully transplanted the mother cat first, then each of her kittens next, one by one, until the family was reunited in the corner of what used to be the farm's living room, a few yards from the woodstove.

Of course, she realized she could only let the fire blaze as long as she was around to tend it. It'd be better if she got the furnace turned on—however that was supposed to happen. Would a handyman work? Or did she have to call an HVAC company? And what if no one could come out on Thanksgiving Day? Then again, she reasoned, the little family had survived in the elements. Cats were hardy, especially those born in the winter in Michigan. It felt like a miracle, really. The whole thing. That a stray, female feline had gotten pregnant so late in the year. That she'd carried her litter to term. Birthed them in the snow, cold and alone. Kept them alive. It took a strong mother to do that, no matter the species.

Tatum had a lot of respect for this mother cat—so much so that she realized a name was in order.

"You know who you remind me of?" she asked the mother cat, who now lay prone as her babies suckled. As she waited briefly for a response, Tatum pulled a phonebook from one of the kitchen cabinets. She thumbed to the handymen section before she answered herself. "You remind me of the story of Christmas. A lonely mother, traveling through the cold, starry night, to a stable where she'd have her baby. Sometimes I think animals are closer to God than humans." Tatum paused, eyeing a column of repairmen in the book. She dug her phone from her pocket and tapped in the first number she laid eyes on. Before hitting Send, she looked at the mother cat, who was purring and fast asleep as her littles suckled along. Worn out, all of them, and still something akin to a blessing to Tatum—as though they needed each other. The cats needed her for comfort and shelter. Tatum needed them, too. To feed her soul and to move along her dream. Tatum finished her thought. "So, you really do. You remind me of the story of Christmas." Then she laughed to herself. "Well, I suppose that's because it's freezing out and Christmas is officially the next holiday. When we were little, our mom let us start decorating for

Christmas on Thanksgiving night. She always said the wait was the best thing about Christmas, and I happen to agree. Anyway, you're a little like Mary, a lost, young mother-to-be with one goal—to keep her newborn baby safe. But actually, it turns out you're going to share your babies with the world. You don't even know that yet, Mama." Tatum spoke softly because the mother looked to be asleep. At the very least, resting her eyes. "Yes. You rest up. You're safe here on this farm with me."

She turned her attention back to her phone to dial the handyman, only to find that the call wouldn't go through.

Out there, on the farm, it would appear that Tatum did not have a cell signal.

CHAPTER 8—CADENCE

Once in their hospital room, Cadence turned antsy. The doctor hadn't been in yet, and they were relying just on nurses to monitor Darla's progress. Even with Pitocin, she wasn't progressing.

It looked like she'd have to go in for a C-section after all. This in and of itself made Cadence all the more nervous, plus—Tatum.

Tatum wasn't answering her phone. With each call that went to voice mail, she grew increasingly more paranoid.

After a nurse came in to declare the doctor was scrubbing in, Darla asked Cadence, "Is she on her way?" She didn't mean their mother, either, who already was on her way.

Cadence chewed her lower lip. "Bad service—I'm just going to step out for a quick second."

Darla seemed unperturbed, but inside, Cadence was roiling in anger at their youngest sister. She punched the Dial icon for the millionth time, and for the millionth time it went straight to voice mail. In all likelihood, Tatum's phone had died and she hadn't even noticed.

Unwilling to just accept that Tatum might miss the birth of their first nieces or nephews, Cadence tried plan B—calling Mila, who was at home and could probably locate Tatum.

Mila answered after the first ring. "Well?" she asked, excitement filling her voice and warming Cadence over.

"No babies yet," Cadence began before faltering awkwardly. Sure, Mila understood how Tatum could be, but that didn't stave off an ounce of embarrassment that Cadence needed help tracking her down. Ridiculous, probably, but Cadence's nervousness was peaking. "We can't get in touch with Tatum. I'm sure she's *fine*—" Cadence suddenly realized that her worry wasn't only for Darla and the birth but also for Tatum. Then again, she couldn't actually remember the last time Tatum's phone *hadn't* gone to voice mail because Tatum never had her phone with her. Normally, she left it plugged in on the kitchen bar. Tatum wasn't a phone person. But she had promised to keep her phone on and with her, so where was she? What had happened?

Mila's reply, however, didn't help to ease Cadence's addled mind. "She's not at the hospital already?" Quick proof that Tatum wasn't at Cadence's house, but nothing to suggest she wasn't at her own house.

"Mila, can you run next door and see if she's asleep? Maybe she took a nap and let her phone die." If that were the case, Cadence would be enraged. Tatum knew better. For her to go promptly to sleep after they'd left—inexcusable. But then, what about the Bait Shop kittens? Did Tatum have cell service out there? Surely she did.

"Going now," Mila answered, and Cadence could hear her moving out the door. She waited several moments until her youngest stepdaughter came back on the line. "No one's answering."

"The spare is beneath the poinsettia plant. Go on in."

"Are you sure? What if—"

"Go ahead, Mila. Darla's about to go into the operating room. They're doing a C-section."

"Oh, gosh." Mila shuffled around on her end of

the line, and Cadence could hear the door creak open before she called out to Tatum once, twice, thrice. A moment passed, then more calling. More moments passed, with more calling out. "She's not here," Mila said at last. "Didn't she go into town?"

"Yes. The Bait Shop. I'll call there."

"Where was she going after the Bait Shop? Is there anything I can do to help?"

Cadence flicked a glance at Darla, who was shifting uncomfortably on the bed. They held each other's gaze through the window, and Cadence could see Darla knew the verdict. Tatum had flaked out. Suddenly, Darla winced. Her hand flew down below her stomach, and she twisted her whole body to the right, away from Cadence.

"Mila, I've gotta go. Find Tatum and tell her to get her butt over here *now*. Please."

Cadence hung up and went to her sister's bedside, where she pushed the nurse's call button over and over again, like a petulant child at a doorbell they couldn't hear ringing. She squeezed Darla's shoulder and fretted and searched the doorway until a scrub-clad nurse appeared.

"Oh, thank goodness. She's in pain. I think something might be wrong," Cadence reported, but she needn't have because Darla was now gritting her teeth and grunting, her features knotted up on her face.

A second figure appeared behind the nurse in the door. The doctor. Once he made his appearance and checked Darla, whose grunts threatened the threshold of wails, things moved quickly. They gave Darla a hair cover and two unfamiliar nurses wheeled her out.

Cadence was left to sit and wait in Darla's assigned hospital room, where she continued to try Tatum's phone.

Finally, fifteen minutes in, Mila called her. "I found Tatum. She didn't have service. Here she is."

Tatum came on the phone. "Cadence, I'm *so* sorry. I was here, at the farm."

"Tatum, listen. Darla's in the operating room. C-section. Can you get here fast? Tatum, you're missing it." It was a guilt trip of the highest order, but *come on*. They all fully expected Tatum to ditch, and here she was, out of service and on the island.

"Of course, I'll get there fast." Tatum sounded out of breath, and Cadence could hear Mila in the background. "I gotta give Mila her phone back. Mine works now! I'm on my way!"

CHAPTER 9—DARLA

Darla awoke in her hospital room with very little memory of the previous hour or more. In fact, she wasn't sure how long she'd been asleep. It was only when her eyes focused on the nearest figure—a woman—that it occurred to her she'd had her babies.

She started up too fast, and her insides cramped hard. Holding back the moan, Darla searched the room only briefly before her eyes fell upon a set of matching hospital bassinets. From within each a classic white swaddling blanket and one pink-and-blue-striped, hospital-issue cotton cap peeked out. Darla fell back, her hand to her chest, relief flooding her whole body and staving off the cramps that swelled inside of her. "Thank you, God," she whispered.

"Wha—?" The bleary-eyed figure stirred from the plastic bench at the far side of the room. Her mother.

She'd made it. Darla smiled but wondered where Cadence and Tatum were. Cadence, the dearheart who wouldn't leave her side. Who'd probably argued with the doctor about being let into the operating room until it had become clear the C-section had gone from back-up plan to emergency. And Tatum, who couldn't be counted on for much, but who *certainly* must have made it in time for the birth.

Darla ignored her stretching mother for the moment and scootched upright, peering in on her babies. She had missed everything so far—their exit from her womb, their gender reveals, the first shots and measurements. She had a feeling that they were a pair of sweet little boys, but it wasn't until she read the placards at the foot of their bassinets that she confirmed this. Little Boy Sageberry 1 and Little Boy Sageberry 2. Darla melted. *Boys*. She looked up at her mom. "Boys?"

Pat Sageberry yawned, smiled, and nodded. "*Boys*. I don't know a thing about raising boys."

Darla might have said the same thing, but she

had a feeling that didn't matter now. Boy or girl, these were her children, and at their core, they were her little humans first. Girl or boy didn't matter. All that mattered was that Darla's dream had come true.

Pulling the nearest bassinet closer, she wondered if she was allowed to just...reach in and pull the baby out.

Before she could do that, her mother stood and approached, sitting at the foot of Darla's bed. "How are you feeling?" Pat asked Darla but kept her eyes on the babies. "They're perfect," she added without waiting for an answer.

"They're perfect," Darla murmured. "I'm okay. Are they okay?" She asked this with every bit of trepidation she felt, but her mom nodded ardently.

"They're more than okay. They are healthy and *perfect*."

Darla hesitated, her hands still on the edge of the first bassinet. She couldn't pick up one baby and not the other. She'd forever remember that moment as some indicator of favoritism. Some inadvertent act that would take root in her heart and influence the upbringing of her children.

"Can you get a nurse?" she asked.

"Why? What's wrong?" Pat frowned and rose

abruptly, moving to the button at the right side of Darla's bed.

"Nothing's wrong. I want to do skin-to-skin," she answered. "But at the exact same time."

"I love that idea." Cadence's voice floated in from the doorway. She stood juggling three cafeteria trays. "Here, I'll help."

Pat and Cadence each carefully lifted a baby onto Darla's chest, sheathing her with a blanket as Darla breathed in the newborn smell. Intoxicating. "Should I feed them? Do I do that now?"

Pat just smiled. "You do whatever feels right."

This answer fell flat for both Darla and Cadence, though. "Are you sure?" Cadence looked at Pat. "Why don't I go see if that one nurse is around. She's a breastfeeding specialist, I think." She looked back at Darla. "They gave the babies formula about an hour ago. You had indicated that was okay. On your birth plan. Is it?"

"I guess." Darla didn't know what was okay. It was as though she'd suddenly lost all decision-making ability. She felt paralyzed with fear and confusion and a sudden rush of insecurity she didn't know she had. But regardless of the logistics of being in the hospital and having new lives to care for, there was one thing that felt utterly natural and perfect. Holding two warm little bodies in her arms.

"Darla, what are you thinking for names?" her mom asked gently.

Cadence left to get a nurse and Pat helped Darla unwrap the babies and cuddle them against her chest. Skin-on-skin proved to be cathartic, and Darla was beginning to think maybe she could feel her way through all of this. Maybe she didn't need permission to do things. Maybe she didn't need a plan, either. She could just...go with it?

"Names?" she wondered aloud.

Darla waited until Cadence returned with the nurse, who helped show her how to position the babies so that they could eat at the same time. Once they were off to a tentative start, Darla finished her answer to her mother. "Strong names. Significant ones." Naturally, she had a short list in mind, but now that she was gazing upon the very lives of her two new sons, nothing on that list rang true. *Kaden, Aiden, Hayden, Braden.* Beautiful names, each of those, and it'd be hard to part with them, but she could see in her suckling sons' eyes that they weren't Kadens or Bradens.

"Maybe this is insensitive, but have you considered naming either of them for their father? Hunter?" Cadence asked.

Darla had already given great thought to Hunter's role in her children's existence, and though any boy might like to have Hunter as either a first or last name—not a terrible idea for a poor kid stuck with Sageberry for a surname—the truth of the matter was that Hunter wasn't part of this. No, he wasn't inconsequential, and Darla hoped someday he'd want to meet his offspring, but he wasn't here now, and he didn't want a part of it, so he didn't deserve the honor. "I have thought about it, but no." The boys' eyes had flickered; they were done nursing and were now sleeping soundly on her chest. It was the warmest, most loving feeling in the world, but still, Darla wasn't sure what to do next. Other than name them, of course.

"Understandable. I didn't think you would, but..." Cadence's voice trailed off.

Struck by the paralysis of the next thing to do and the best names to give her babies, Darla opted to change the conversation entirely. "Where's Tatum?"

Cadence and Pat shared a look.

"I mean, obviously she isn't *here*." At that moment Darla realized how famished she felt. She could eat a dozen doughnuts without being sated, she thought. And with that, her focus shifted from caring about where Tatum was to what food Cadence had brought on those trays...

"She tried to make it, sweetheart," Pat cooed, sitting at Darla's side and rubbing small circles into the back of the baby on the right. "She'll be here soon, though. Isn't that right, Cadence?"

Darla looked at Cadence, who pursed her lips. "Hopefully."

"Well, as long as she's on her way." Darla kissed the top of each baby's head. "I'll wait to name these little guys until Tatum gets here. But for now, can I eat something?"

CHAPTER 10—TATUM

Tatum stood at the Heirloom Island marina, a modest dock that normally rocked up and down with the tides of Lake Huron. But now, with a thin sheet of ice creeping out from the bank like an icicle slowly forming, the dock was stiff across the water. Snow had fallen off and on in the last hour since Tatum had been in touch with her sisters, and by now, the *Birch Bell* should have arrived. It was long past due, and Tatum had begun to worry.

She bit her lip and shivered and twisted her body, thinking all at once of the myriad things she was juggling just then. Her own dogs—who normally didn't have to deal with long periods away from human company—had taken a back seat to the new cat family, who were alone and probably freezing in the farmhouse. Not as freezing as if they were in a box behind the Bait Shop, but still cold. That place was a veritable icebox. Of course, ahead of both of these very real concerns was Darla, who'd already gone into labor and was probably done with the whole thing by now, and Tatum—stupid Tatum—had *missed* it.

After waiting as long as she had, it finally occurred to Tatum to go into the little wooden box of a marina office to ask after the ferry.

"Excuse me?" she asked of the bored-looking, bundled-up teenager who scrolled through his phone even as she addressed him. With a grunt for acknowledgment, he didn't elicit much hope in Tatum, but she pressed on. "Any word about the ferry? Still running late?"

This brought about a snort from the kid, who finally spared her a brief glance. "It's not running at all. Didn't you see?" He made a vague gesture with his phone beyond Tatum toward the dock. "I'm only here for emergency vessels."

Tatum dutifully followed his wave to find nothing more than a continuous, slowly falling curtain of snowflakes, like the gauzy drapes hanging in her sister's house on the boardwalk. "See what?" Tatum asked blankly.

"You're the only one here."

Tatum frowned. "So? I bet people are trying to come here from the mainland. And the ferry runs on a schedule, not on appointments. Or—waitlists."

"Lady." The teenager cleared his throat and suddenly sounded older than he appeared. "That schedule depends on more than your last-minute Thanksgiving plans. It depends on weather, lake conditions, and vessel conditions."

Tatum sighed. "Do you know when it'll be running again?"

But all he could do was shrug, returning his image to that of an underpaid, indifferent wage-worker with too many smartphone apps and too little responsibility.

Tatum didn't know the first thing about driving a boat, or else she'd go find an old island fisherman and pay him whatever he wanted to take his boat out for the day. That's when it occurred to her. She didn't have to drive a boat to get a private ride to Birch Harbor. She just needed to *know* a private boat owner.

And she did. She knew two of them, in fact.

It took Tatum another fifteen minutes to get back to the house and search frantically for his phone number. Mason Acton. Naturally, the slip of paper he'd left Darla was pinned to the fridge with a magnet, a memento of the before-times, in Tatum's mind. Before they'd come to terms with Darla's delicate state, and before Tatum had realized the acquisition of her business property—and maybe one-day home.

"Hey." Tatum didn't wait for him to greet her before launching into her problem. "I need a ride to the mainland. Are you free? I know you're probably at dinner with your family or something, but—"

"Whoa, whoa, whoa. Tatum, slow *down*. What's going on? Is everything okay? Is it Darla?"

Of course, it was Darla. Tatum tried hard not to roll her eyes on her end of the line. But a thought seized Tatum midsentence. This was not her news to tell. It was Darla's. Darla had even wanted to keep it all very quiet. Almost secret-level quiet. And of everyone in the world Darla had *not* wanted to know about this, Mason was top of that list. Tatum was about to screw up royally. Even more royally than she already had. "It's—" She swallowed and thought fast and hard—and thinking fast and hard was a real problem for someone like Tatum, a silly heart without a care in the world—except for when it came to animals, of course. Her brain flipped and slid in her head while she made up a perfectly reasonable follow-up request to her alarm. "Um, Darla's *great*. It's *not* Darla. It's—me!" And it *was* Tatum, who needed help, that was. "I need help. I'm not okay."

"Oh." Mason sounded...confused at best. Suspicious and vaguely weirded out at worst. "What's wrong, Tatum?" His sympathy was less than believable, but she didn't blame him for that.

"I'm fine! I mean—everything is okay. I just need a ride is all." She winced at her own awkwardness. "I forgot to buy the turkey." She slapped the side of her head, hoping it was loud enough for Mason to hear and therefore truly believe her, that she'd simply forgotten to buy the turkey for Thanksgiving. "Bait Shop's plumb out of 'em. Turkeys, I mean."

"You haven't gotten a turkey yet? It's...Thanksgiving Day, Tatum."

"I know! And we've got everything else. The pudding"—*pudding?*—"the stuffing, the vegetables. And the buns!" She was feeling manic and frantic and crazed. "The buns are already out of the oven, too!" Tatum swallowed a big gulp. She was so close to giving it all away. She'd better shut up.

"Is that—"

"Never mind the buns; we need a turkey, and I have to get into town to buy one."

"Tatum, they'll be frozen. You won't have time to thaw them out. Are you—are you *sure* everything is okay?"

"Mason, can you drive out here and give me a ride into town, or can't you?" Tatum put on her determined face—for herself since he couldn't see it.

"I'm with my family in Detroit, Tatum, but if it's an emergency, you could call the marine patrol. I have a buddy who—"

"It's not an emergency, it's just urgent. I can't call marine patrol for a turkey." She laughed wildly and paced the floor and silently cursed herself for rescuing the cat family all while cursing Darla for going and having surprise twins and—

"I'm so sorry, Darla. If it's not an emergency...I mean, if you can wait until this afternoon, I can come?"

"No, *no*. I can't do that to you. You're not at my family's beckon hall."

"Beckon hall?"

"We can't expect you to drop everything just

because I messed up." She was brainstorming every other avenue to get to the mainland, but it was beginning to matter less and less. With every passing minute, Tatum was farther away from her sisters and the babies and everything that should have mattered *more* to her.

"Beckon hall? You mean *beck and call*?" Tatum detected the hint of a smile in his voice, but she knew it wasn't for her. It was for Darla. Mason cared about the whole family, sure. They were all friends together, sure. But it was Darla he asked after first. Darla who mattered to him.

Not Tatum.

But could she blame him? No. Why would anyone care about the girl who only cared about animals?

CHAPTER 11—CADENCE

It wasn't until the morning after the delivery that Tatum managed to catch the ferry over to the mainland. Cadence would have gone to retrieve her, but she didn't want to leave Darla or the babies alone for that long. Their mother was there, but she kept drifting in and out of sleep, and Cadence figured it was best to let her rest anyway.

Cadence now returned to their assigned hospital room with two Styrofoam cups, hers with hazelnut creamer and her mother's black. "Here, Mom." She passed the cup over and rejoined Darla at the bed, lowering onto the waffle-patterned hospital blanket. It was stiff and it served only to remind Cadence of those final moments with Hendrik. Everything seemed to remind Cadence of Hendrik, and that didn't change even with the emergence of new life. Even with the emergence of *two* new lives.

"Is she here yet?" Darla asked, scanning through the open door. Tatum should arrive any moment, and Darla was the most excited to see her, much to Cadence's annoyance. Of course, Cadence should also be excited that Tatum would *finally* make it to the hospital, but it was hard not to hold even the slightest grudge after Cadence had repeatedly counseled the youngest of the three sisters to *keep her phone on* and *be ready*. Oh well. At least Cadence was here. At least, Cadence thought, she had the opportunity to be here. Had all this happened a mere one year earlier, Cadence may not have even been in the loop on any pregnancy.

Their mother answered Darla through a yawn. "Let me just check my phone to see if she's texted or called." A beat later, Pat looked up, her eyes heavy but flashing anew. "She's here. She's in the lobby signing in. They'll call."

Cadence shot up from the bed. "I'll go get her and bring her in."

Once all four Sageberry women were reunited together in Darla's room and after Tatum had cooed over Darla's bravery and beauty and strength, she turned her wonderment to the babies in their plastic bassinets. "They're so cute. I mean *really* cute." Tatum looked very seriously upon Darla. Almost with concern. "I had no idea babies could be so cute."

"You mean as cute as, say, *kittens*?" Cadence couldn't stifle her laugh. Tatum, despite her aloofness and general inability to be accountable, was as sincere as they came. The love Tatum had for her new nephews was palpable. Contagious. But Cadence had already caught the bug long ago. As soon as it had been way too late for Cadence—when Darla had taken the brown paper bag and returned with a positive pregnancy test.

"We were talking about names," Pat said, easing the conversation back to one of the most important moments of the day. *Names.* Cadence loved names. She'd have had a million children if only to name them. Once, she'd had a pet fish who'd given birth, and Cadence had painstakingly tried to track and name every single little squishy baby fish. It hadn't worked out well, as they'd been even harder to tell apart than Darla's boys, but little Cadence had tried.

She looked fondly at the babies now. "What about William, after Dad?" she ventured delicately. William wouldn't be Cadence's first pick. She'd name a baby Henry or even Henderson—something close to Hendrik's name. That was *if* she even got pregnant by some act of miraculous force right now. If Hendrik were still around, any boy child they had would surely carry their father's name, at least in a small way—maybe as a middle name? Cadence added, "You could pick any middle name. You could even call him 'Billy' or 'Will'—unlike Dad." Their father had gone by Bill. "Or he could go by a middle name?"

Darla nodded. "William. Definitely. For a middle name, though. I had something else in mind for their first names." Darla stared lovingly at her precious twins.

"You already have names?" their mother asked.

"Well, sure she does. She probably had names when she was twelve. In fact," Tatum pointed out, "I distinctly remember that Darla kept one of those paperback books with baby names and toted it around like a dictionary or some reference material. Why did you do that?"

Darla smiled. "I couldn't wait to have babies and give them names." She shrugged.

Cadence let out a willowy sigh. "I know what you mean. And I remember that. Remember we named our dolls? Each one had, like, five names. Every last Barbie doll. Every last baby doll." What would it have been like to mother a little girl? Cadence, for all she'd done with Fay, Lotte, and Mila, hadn't been there when they were that young. She'd had her mother-daughter experiences with her sisters, insofar as that had ever happened. Mainly, the trio had just been sisters.

"No. Well—*yes*. I actually did have names picked out. But I've changed my mind." Darla scooted up and pulled each bassinet closer to her, studying her sons thoughtfully.

"So you *do* have names picked, or you *don't*?" Tatum scratched her head, looking bewildered. Cadence turned back to Darla.

"I'm confused, too. You *have* names, then?"

"I was hoping to have a little help with that, actually," Darla said at last.

"But not William?" Cadence jumped on the opportunity, but she remained uncertain about what Darla wanted. "Do you have something in mind? Or—"

"What about biblical names?" Pat offered.

Darla's eyes flashed. "I like that idea. Especially since—" When she didn't finish her sentence, Cadence and the other two were left to guess what she meant, and it was an easy guess. Darla retained a heavy dose of guilt in the wake of leaving Hunter—

especially since he'd blocked her. Darla would be raising two boys without their father. Potentially without any father figure to speak of since no grandfathers were in the picture—and no uncles.

Not even Hendrik.

"What about Joseph?" Pat said.

"Either boy could be a Joseph," Darla agreed readily. "That quiet strength. And the fact that they're here—even without being asked to be here." She laughed softly. "I'm making no sense."

"I get it. As much as you brought them into the world, they made a dream come true for you, right?" Cadence lowered onto the foot of the bed and rested her hand on Darla's sheathed legs.

Tears welled up in the new mother's eyes. "They're like my own little Nativity. And yes, Cadence. They're sort of—going to have guide me, I think. Through this. I'm going to need a lot of guidance, in fact." Darla looked up, and panic streaked across her face suddenly.

"You feel lost, don't you?" Tatum neared the bed and gripped the footboard, staring at Darla hard. "Like a lost sheep."

Darla didn't meet Tatum's gaze. She pinned her eyes on the boys again and nodded slowly.

Tatum rounded the footboard and lowered her

body to the other side of the bed. "Look at this one," she said, poking her finger into his fist. "Like a miniature shepherd holding his staff." The baby's eyes opened momentarily, searching blearily until they settled on Darla. "Looking for his sheep."

"A shepherd," Darla murmured, running her finger up the chubby cheek of the boy with his finger curled around Tatum's.

Cadence felt a sob crawl up her throat, but she quickly looked at the other baby, searching for something there. Some meaning. Some clue. It hit her. "Look. This one is a little towhead. And his downy hair sort of rings around like a halo."

"Like an angel," Darla murmured, now holding the second baby's little fist.

"I have it," Cadence said, brightening. "Shepard." She nodded to the baby who held on to Tatum's thumb, then nodded to the baby with a halo of wispy blond hair. "And Gabriel."

CHAPTER 12—DARLA

When, only one week later, Darla and the boys were discharged from the hospital, she was hesitant to go. She sat on the edge of her bed. Her mother and Cadence flanked her, each holding one infant car seat. Pat was assigned Shepard, and Cadence was assigned Gabriel. In the end, it had been Cadence and Pat who stayed the week at the hospital with Darla, taking turns sleeping on the roll-away cot as the other slept on a narrow window bench. Tatum had gone home but had visited daily between her bouts of setting up her new business. Whenever the Sageberrys weren't talking about Darla and the babies, they listened to Tatum wax poetic about vacuuming baseboards and scrubbing a clawfoot tub with a pumice stone. For Tatum, who'd never been much of a home project person, it was all hard labor and impressive work to be proud of. To brag and complain about in one breath.

Even when Tatum wasn't at the hospital, though, it was cramped—three women and two babies proved to be about four people too many for one tiny recovery room.

Still, when the nurse came in with discharge paperwork and postoperative instructions and tips and tricks for new moms and yadda yadda...Darla was not ready to go. She could sleep on the sliver of a window bench seat or a roll-away cot. She could maybe stay there, and the babies could go to the nursery.

But the babies were dressed in their sweet little unisex, going-home outfits. Cadence had curled Darla's hair, and Pat had given her a tube of mascara to swipe on so that she felt herself again. None of it really helped. Her stomach was almost as big as it was *before* the boys had come out of there. Her ankles were as thick as tree trunks. Residual gas pockets cramped up her torso clear into her chest. Her neck hurt from sleeping at the slight hospital-bed angle.

Going home would fix all of this, of course. All of

these ailments. And yet Darla wasn't ready. Breastfeeding hurt. The babies seemed to sleep only when Darla was wide awake and unable to rest herself, thereby discounting the wild notion that new mothers should *sleep when baby does!*

"Any other questions?" The nurse asked this with a tender expression. Was she a mother? Did she *get* it?

"Um—" Darla frowned and searched the room for a question to ask. Something to do with talcum powder—was that still a thing?—or burp cloths or nipple salve? What about that feeding schedule, too? So far, the nurses had prompted almost every nursing session, with just a couple of exceptions when it felt natural to Darla to bring the boys to her bosom. But, see, that was the problem—she felt natural only about twenty-five percent of the time. The other seventy-five percent? Decidedly unnatural. Awkward. Ill-prepared, and maybe even reckless.

"I have a question," Pat interrupted.

"Grandmas have questions, too," the nurse replied with a wink at Darla as if there was some joke she was missing. Darla wasn't in the mood for jokes.

"How long should she stay home from work?

We've told Darla at least four weeks—that's how long I stayed home with the girls. Er—well, maybe it was three weeks with Tatum. She was such a tiny thing. I sneezed, and out she came!" Pat roared. Darla cringed, and Cadence quickly downplayed it all.

"I read that with a C-section, you ought to be home and resting for six weeks," she remarked smugly. Or maybe it wasn't smugness, but there was an edge there that aggravated Darla. She swallowed and considered this. Six weeks would mean she'd miss the Nativity play for sure. Six weeks felt like forever, but it also felt too short. They were complicated, these new-mother feelings. On the one hand, she'd very much like to stay in the hospital for the duration of the six weeks. On the other hand, she'd like to go back to work the very next day.

"Six weeks is a great goal, but with multiples, recovery can take longer," the nurse replied gently. "Darla, the doctor will write a note to excuse you from work for eight weeks to start. He usually reevaluates after that."

"Eight weeks?" Darla panicked internally. Eight weeks of staying home and resting? No heading into school to grade or lesson plan or tutor or anything?

"That's a suggestion, though, right? I could return sooner? If I felt well enough?"

"You really shouldn't rush your recovery, sweetheart," her mom said by way of encouragement. It was not encouraging, though. Nothing felt encouraging to Darla in that moment.

By sheer force of will, she pushed up from the bed and followed her mother and sister and her two newborn sons to the hall. There, a wheelchair awaited Darla.

"If I need a wheelchair, should I really be going home?" she asked no one in particular.

Light laughter came as a reply and before she knew it, Darla was wheeled out of the hospital and into her mother's waiting car. From there, the remainder of the trip home was a blur. Darla tended to the boys the whole way, worried sick about the littlest hiccup or the mildest fuss. Once they arrived in the house on the boardwalk, Darla started to feel better.

The first night home, Pat stayed with Darla in her bedroom, where they'd pulled together matching bassinets, one on each side of the bed. Darla hated to assign one baby to her mom at all; it felt cruel and neglectful. But by the next morning, nothing mattered.

At some point in the early hours—or earlyish—Cadence entered the room, and this brought about nothing short of a hallucination from Darla.

Confused, she called out to Hunter. This made her mother—also sleep deprived—cry. Cadence, now as confused as Darla, wondered aloud if they should call the doctor, but Pat said no. All Darla needed was sleep. It would fix everything.

Darla agreed, and Cadence said she'd take the babies, change them, feed them, burp them, and read to them for as long as Darla wanted.

Some hours later, Darla awoke with a start. Unsure at first where she was, it took some moments to feel the body of her mother in the bed next to her. The sunlight streaming in through the gauzy curtains. And if sunlight was streaming in, then it wasn't morning, not in Darla's west-facing bedroom.

She rolled out of bed, sore and bleary-eyed, coming to some vague understanding that she was no longer pregnant. She'd had the babies. They were all home. Her mother was there to help. *This* was the new normal.

Darla found Cadence wide-eyed, watching *Dr. Phil*. The twins were fast asleep on either of her arms. The picture was so perfect, Darla might have taken a photo if she'd had any idea where her phone or a camera was. But she didn't, and reality struck. It should be *her* lounging on the sofa with a baby on each side and a talk show on the television, reminding her just how normal and perfect she was—by comparison to whatever poor sap had made his or her way onto a show meant to reveal the hardest parts of life.

Finding her voice, Darla cleared her throat. "How are they?"

Cadence didn't startle. She just glanced at the babies then looked up. "They're perfect. How are *you*?"

Darla gave herself a moment to assess her body, her mind. An answer followed. "I'm...good. I feel good." She moved to just in front of Cadence and gestured with her arms. "Can I—?"

Cadence started to shuffle but slowed herself so as not to wake the boys. Somehow, she managed to unpeel herself from the sofa while holding both boys, allowing Darla to position herself in the same spot and take them. The boys didn't wake once. *Of course.* Cadence said, "Gabriel fell asleep first. Shepard took a little longer. It was like he knew I was going to watch TV and he wanted to watch with me."

Darla gulped down this morsel of information about Shepard as if it might cue an early personality trait. Maybe he was into storytelling. Maybe he'd be her little thespian. And Gabriel, then? Would he always be an easy sleeper? What did it mean, this burgeoning bit of their behavior?

"So, I've been thinking." Cadence spoke as she moved into the kitchen. "If you think you can't return to work after Christmas break, I could possibly absorb some of your classes. One on my prep. One into my second hour—I only have eight in there. And my fourth hour has just ten kids. I could take yours and make it work, you know—"

Shaking her head vehemently enough for emphasis but not so severely as to disturb the boys, Darla announced, "I'm going back. Maybe before Christmas, even."

"Darla." Cadence swung her head in from the kitchen, a carafe of coffee hooked in her hand. "You can't go back. Not until clear after New Year's. And will you really want to?"

Darla looked down at the boys and pressed her lips gently against the downy head of each. This was the best smell in the world, Darla was sure of it. Maybe Cadence was right. Maybe she wouldn't want to go back to work. And certainly, she wasn't ready now. Even if the prospect of parenting without a partner scared the bejeezus out of Darla, there was no denying she was head over heels in love with these two.

Whereas before their birth—and before learning that there were *two* in there—all Darla had worried about was not having the perfect little family of three.

Now there *were* three of them. And it was just right.

But even so, something tugged at Darla, deep down. And she couldn't be sure if it was a need to give up her career and settle in...or go back to work. To that, however, Darla would have to put into motion the search that she'd put off out of some deluded belief that this mom thing would be *easy*: finding a babysitter. One who wasn't one of her busy sisters.

CHAPTER 13—TATUM

The week Darla returned home with the babies, Tatum really wanted to be there with her. She really did. But the timing was terrible. And Tatum felt *terrible* that the timing was terrible. Really, she did.

But her livelihood and her dream had been put at stake in that week since the kittens had been found and Darla'd had her C-section and Tatum's nephews joined the family in the little boardwalk house on Heirloom Island.

The Friday of that week, Tatum was expecting the lion's share of her handymen to meet her at the shelter house and get things rolling in earnest. This would include the furnace specialist. Fat chance she could afford a furnace installation, but the stove simply wasn't enough. It would also include a guy who would take a look at structural concerns, like the crack-turned-gap in the kitchen. Lastly, a plumber was due out. There was running water to the property already, so that was a start, but whoever had lived on the farm last hadn't winterized properly, and pipes must have been frozen and busted throughout the house. Leaks sprung at odd spots from the second floor down to the basement, and—this being an island—Tatum had begun to wonder if the place even ought to have a basement at all. How far down did the Heirloom soil really reach? Could one oversized dog bounding down the basement steps manage to punch a hole clear through to Lake Huron? These were the issues invading Tatum's every thought even when she tripped down the stairs to breakfast to find Darla or Cadence half-asleep on the sofa with the babies.

But as soon as the three men left the shelter property, Tatum promised herself she'd give the kittens a quick cuddle then head directly home to help with the night shift. She *promised* herself. And she'd promised Darla, too.

The Manger House

THE PLUMBER SHOWED UP FIRST. A hefty portly fellow with ruddy red cheeks, a pockmarked nose, and a full white beard, he endeared himself to Tatum instantly. He reminded her of Santa Claus, actually. He set about hunting down the cracked pipes, calling in a modest crew of underlings an hour into it. With any luck, the plumber claimed, they'd have the pipes all fixed up and ready for winter and whatever else Tatum and her new property could spring on him.

As he and his men worked, she tended the kittens, letting them climb over her and cuddle in her lap while she searched an old phonebook for other animal shelter names to get some ideas. That lead her to make a list of things she needed to do ASAP. Buy a domain and start a website bleh. Consider employees and shift schedules and…it was a lot. Of course, this was all information she ought to have looked into well before she ponied up a down payment and took on a mortgage, but here she was. There was no going back now.

Nothing felt right as she thought and thought. Her previous research had suggested that shelters were often established by groups—animal rights' activists, veterinarians with a penchant for charity work, and sometimes families who had lots of extra money and no other way to honor pets they'd lost to the rainbow bridge.

Tatum, however, was just a loner. A single woman with a pack of her own feisty pets and two sisters who had better things to do than build a shelter up, brick by brick. But it wasn't until the furnace guy showed up, ran a quick estimate, and proved to Tatum that she couldn't afford central heat that hopelessness began to set in. She couldn't afford the things she needed in order to make this a legitimate establishment—nonprofit or otherwise.

And if it wasn't bad before, the repair company sent out an errand boy at ten to five. He trudged muddy snow into the farmhouse while explaining they had an emergency at the Koken and wouldn't be able to send someone out until the following Friday. Tatum nearly decided to hold him hostage and make the boy help her anyway. He'd trekked all that way just to deliver a message. Might as well stick around and pitch in. But the plumber rejoined her just as soon as the boy scurried out, not bothering to take his mud with him.

"You're all up and running. Or the water is," the plumber said, breaking her thoughts after she'd fielded the bad-news visit.

"Oh, great." Tatum brightened only slightly. "That's one thing down."

"What else do you need, if ya don't mind my askin'?"

She sighed. What *didn't* need doing? The house repairs, the heat, opening the shelter for real, placing the kittens—which she hadn't even thought about, truth be told. And then, of course, her family down on the boardwalk. Her nephews and Darla should be her priority, but here she was, shivering in an abandoned old farmhouse with a stray mama cat, a jovial plumber, and her own pets at home to feed and walk. "Oh, you know," Tatum replied, mustering optimism. "Just a Christmas miracle."

CHAPTER 14—CADENCE

Cadence returned to work the Monday after Darla and the boys came home, but she didn't exactly *want* to return to work quite yet. It wasn't that she had baby fever, necessarily. More like *family* fever. An itch to stick beside the sister she'd nearly lost to a feud just a year before.

But by lunchtime on Monday, it was all Cadence could do to not call out sick for the rest of the school day. She ached to be at home with Darla—doing the dishes and running burp cloths through the laundry. With their mother returning home to Detroit, Darla *really* needed someone available around the clock. Tatum, bless her wild heart, was otherwise preoccupied. Cadence, however, was wholly invested, to the point of devotion. Why shouldn't it be her?

So, come the end of the school day, Cadence marched into the headmaster's office and asked him for an impromptu meeting.

At St. Mary's, the school's leadership was segregated from the leadership of the church, and therefore, involving the priest was unnecessary. At least at this juncture. And anyway, if Father Richard did want to be involved, he'd have to do so privately—not in his role as a patron of the school, but as Cadence's religious and spiritual confidant. It reeked of awkwardness, but Cadence was beyond feeling awkward. She'd moved on to pure desperation to go and stay home and help Darla and the boys. Period, bottom line.

"Mr. McGee," she began, her tone unwavering and her face unflinching. "I'm here to inform you that I'm taking a leave of absence for the remainder of the semester."

Stunned, apparently, Mr. McGee sat slack-jawed and silent for a beat. At last, he replied, "Ms. Van Dam—"

"It's Mrs." Cadence couldn't control her knee-jerk reaction. Very often in the past year, uncomfortable acquaintances, students, parents, and coworkers had started fumbling over her address—was she a Miss again? Still a Mrs.? Sometimes,

Cadence wished she lived in the 1700s and could simply go by Widow Van Dam. That would be the best thing, in her opinion. She didn't apologize for interrupting her boss. She sat still as ice, her fingers laced together in her lap.

He stammered briefly. "So sorry, of course. *Mrs.* Van Dam, is everything all right?"

"Of course," she rushed to answer. "It's just that Darla didn't know about the twins—none of us did." The school community had been exceptional in their show of support. Flowers and baby gifts, even a late-fall baby shower in the staff lounge—it was all generous and thoughtful. And beyond that, they'd told Darla not to worry a bit about returning—that she'd earn out her pay to the end of the semester, and after that, they'd talk things over. See what they could do. It was all too much—too kind, really. And here Cadence was, creating a whole new problem for them on top of losing their English teacher and scrambling for subs.

And still, Cadence struggled to care about that— about St. Mary's, her career there, her coworkers, or even her very own students.

A more perceptive person might have wondered if there wasn't something more to Cadence's sudden attitude shift. But then, *was* it so sudden? She'd left teaching years ago. It was just this year that she'd returned. Perhaps she wasn't ready. Perhaps *that* had been the problem all along? Not that she'd stopped caring once the babies came, but that she'd never cared to begin with.

"Okay," Mr. McGee replied slowly. She could see him thinking through this. She felt hot in her argyle sweater and corduroy pants. Itchy, too. She rose. "Before you go—"

"Yes?" Cadence stood tall, her hands still clasped.

"You will return after Christmas recess, won't you?"

Cadence knew the right answer was yes, of course she would. But deep inside, there was no 'yes' to be found. Only a longing to be at home.

"I HAVE AN IDEA," Cadence declared the moment she stepped into Darla and Tatum's house next door.

Darla sat on the sofa, nursing the boys and watching a soap opera. "Really?" She perked up, sacrificing the show for whatever Cadence was going to say. Cadence knew it had better be good. Not because Darla was missing the soap opera to hear her out, but because Darla had it made in the shade in the second house on the boardwalk. There was no reason for her—in her mind, probably—to make a change. Unless that change—Cadence feared—was moving home to Detroit and closer to Hunter and their mom and farther away from Cadence and the island and the life they were making together...

"Move in with me. Next door."

Darla shifted so suddenly that Shepard, identifiable by the blue baby hat rather than the green one that Gabriel wore, unlatched and wailed. This, in turn, caused Gabriel to also unlatch and wail, and soon enough Cadence regretted her timing terribly.

The babies cried and cried, and Darla fussed over them as they fussed back at her. Cadence swooped in, picking up the green-hatted baby—Gabriel. "Shh, shh, shh, shh." She directed Darla, "Get Shep back on, then we'll add Gabe."

But Darla was in tears. "No," she said, weeping miserably as she held the blue-capped baby against her. "It's no use. When one goes, both go. It's impossible—two against one. I'm outnumbered." And then, more quietly, "I deserve it."

"Deserve what?"

Tatum appeared, disheveled and grinning from ear to ear, but her grin slipped away as she met Cadence's worried gaze. "What happened?" She lifted her chin and searched for the baby cradled in Darla's arms, but Cadence was quick to assuage her.

"Nothing happened. Darla's exhausted. That's all."

Darla let out a final, shuddering sob, confirming Cadence's evaluation of the situation.

"Oh, Darla," Tatum said, falling onto the sofa and gently pulling Shepard from her arms. "Let me take him. Go upstairs and sleep. It's still the afternoon. You can get a great nap in before dinner."

Cadence chewed her lower lip. *Dinner*. She hadn't made any solid plans yet. She was hoping Tatum could cook tonight, but she wasn't quite ready for Darla to leave after all.

She rubbed Gabriel's back as he hiccuped himself to sleep. "Think it over, okay?"

"Think what over?" Tatum echoed, looking from Cadence to Darla and back again.

Darla answered for both of them. "Cadence says maybe I should move back in with her." She frowned, then added, "Which I guess means she'd want you to move, too?"

"But my dogs. And Charm. You don't want pets at your house, I thought. And, wait a second, wait a second. *Move?* Why? We're fine, right? Here, I mean? In our own place?" Then Tatum's face pinched harder in panic. "Is it money? Do we need to pay you more for rent or something?"

"No!" Cadence practically shouted the word, but baby-holding instincts kicked in and it came out as a hoarse stage whisper. "No." She swallowed and shook her head. "It's not about money. We're getting a good rate from the rental next door." She nodded toward the third boardwalk house, which she'd converted to a long-term rental that fall—easily, too. Turned out there was a dearth of available apartments or houses for rent on the island. "It's not money." This was true. And besides, she still had her hand in the cookie jar of event hosting. She just... hadn't given much time to that. Between teaching— assuming she stayed on—the rental property, and what Darla and Tatum were paying, she was doing more than fine. Of course, if Darla and Tatum moved out, she'd up the rent, but that was neither here nor there.

"It's Darla I'm worried about."

"I'm a new mom. I'm tired, but I'm *fine*."

"You're not fine; you need *help*." Tatum was fierce with sympathy. She rocked Shepard in her arms and shushed him, but it was entirely ineffectual. His fussing ramped back up until Darla recovered him from Tatum and held him against her again.

"Even if I were with Hunter, he'd be at work. Just like you two are. I can manage. It's hard, but I can manage."

Tatum asked innocently, "What about when you go back to work?"

"You mean the Nativity play? Do you think I can do it still?" Darla brightened, and it was clear her heart leapt. Cadence felt terrible for her. She could see clear as day how important it was for Darla to return to the classroom. How she was polar opposite to Cadence, who feared being away from home. Who feared interacting with people these days. Darla *needed* them.

"You can't go back until after Christmas," Cadence whispered.

"She could do the play. It's just after school," Tatum pointed out.

Cadence smirked, but Darla was aflame with excitement, patting Shepard too quickly and talking a mile a minute. "Maybe I can't teach, but I can do rehearsals for an hour a day. I could easily do that." She looked at Cadence. "You can be home at 3:30?"

"Yes, but it's still early, Dar."

"I'll talk to the doctors, but if one of you can be here with the babies, then it'll work."

"I'll be here," Cadence volunteered hesitantly,

but only because she hadn't yet told her sisters she was on leave, effective today. No time like the present. "I'll be here all day, every day until after the break, actually."

"Why?" Tatum and Darla asked at once.

"I told Mr. McGee I'm going on family leave to help you." She waited for a response.

Tatum and Darla exchanged a look, and Cadence felt a little sick when she couldn't read it. Like a desperate woman in the face of a man she wanted to impress but was failing miserably to do so. "What?" she pressed.

"You can't do that, Cadence." Tatum said it, but Darla's face agreed readily.

"Yes, I can. And I did. Darla needs the help. If Hunter were here, he'd take off work."

"Not six weeks. Not even two weeks, probably," Darla replied. "And how can the school function with two of us gone?"

Tatum held up her hands in an X symbol. "I am *not* teaching algebra. Or addition, for that matter. And I'm *definitely* not teaching Shakespeare. To do or not to do is *not* even a question."

Cadence had no laugh to give even though Tatum had somewhat handled an expression well, for once. She was stressed to the max now, to not have her sisters' support even though all she was trying to do was support them. Both of them. With Cadence home, Tatum could work on the shelter. She said this aloud, pointing a finger behind Gabriel's back. "You won't be here."

"Cadence," Darla said, her voice wobbly, "are you *sure* about this?"

"I'm sure," Cadence replied. "I already talked to McGee. It's a done deal. We'll be back in January. You and me."

But all three of them knew that this wasn't the solution, either. Because if all three were at work, then what about the babies? They couldn't go to the school. For one, it wasn't productive. More than that, though, it wasn't safe. Not with adolescent germs and whatnot. And they couldn't go with Tatum to the property at the south end of the island. Besides, Tatum would be distracted. She'd make a bad babysitter. It was either Darla or Cadence.

"All we have to worry about is *after* Christmas recess. For now, Darla and I are at home. Tatum, you can keep working on the shelter. That's your focus, and that's okay." Cadence said this with all the confidence she could muster.

They put the matter to rest, and Tatum took over on dinner, bringing Cadence up to speed on the slow improvements of the farm property and the alarming growth of the kittens. Darla rested upstairs, and the babies cooed in their playpen, on their backs, staring up at the toys Cadence waved over them.

"Next week, I hope to roll out some information materials. Plus, I'm getting the rest of the repairs done. The ones I can afford, at least."

"Do you need help?" Cadence asked.

"With what? Repairs? Yes. But I'm in contact with a great company and—"

"I mean cash, Tate."

Tatum looked at her, her cheeks flushed. "No. You've helped enough. Seriously, Cadence. And anyway, you'll be here with Darla."

Cadence nodded.

Tatum read something in her because she asked, "What is it?"

"Nothing!" Cadence said airily, scooping up Shepard and peeking into his diaper to confirm a change was in order. "I just—I think I might not go back after Christmas break." There. She'd said it. Out loud. To another human being. A sister, at that.

Tatum made a choking noise. "Why!?"

"What else are we going to do, Tatum?" Cadence

The Manger House

hissed, hoping Darla couldn't hear. Darla didn't need that kind of stress right now; she really didn't.

"What do you mean? We're going to—" Her mouth froze midsentence. "Ohhh. The babies. Well, we talked about that. Darla was going to find a babysitter. Someone like Mila."

"But Mila left." Cadence sighed over this. She was so happy for Mila but so sad for herself. And now for Darla and the boys. No one had even broached the subject of Mila's leaving and how it would shift their plans for the balance of the school year. Surely Darla was obsessed with the thought, but she hadn't said a word.

Tatum clicked her tongue and shook her head. "It's a hard spell. Made harder by the cold weather."

Cadence finished with the diaper change and returned Shepard to the playpen. "What does cold weather have to do with it?" She glanced outside. Snow fell in a soft, white curtain, clouding over her view of the lake. A roaring fire would do just now, but Cadence didn't have the energy for it. None of them did.

"Well, I'll tell you, it makes it hard to get anything done on the farm."

"Are you going to keep on calling it that?" Cadence wondered half-heartedly. It could be a cute name for an animal shelter, or it could be an off-putting one. "If you call it The Farm, people are going to think it's a funny farm, where wayward animals are sent out to pasture."

"No." Tatum popped her head in from the kitchen. "But I do need a name."

"Just call it Heirloom Island Animal Sanctuary and be done. Or Animal Shelter. Or Rescue. Right?"

"There's a connotation."

Cadence laughed and left the boys to join Tatum at the stove. "What connotation? Don't you *want* a connotation?"

"I mean—my own animals will be there, too, you know? And I might even offer emergency vet services if I can find one. A vet, I mean. I just think, *yes*, it's a rescue and a shelter, but I want a more meaningful name. This is my *dream*, Cadence. Go home or go big, they say."

"It's 'Go big or go home,' but I get your point. I feel the same way about my events business."

"Have anything planned yet? Something wintry?"

"Well, like you said, the cold weather makes it hard for people to want to get out. Plus, the ferry doesn't run as often. Who wants to come to the island over frozen chunks of Lake Huron?" She looked through the kitchen window to see exactly what she meant. It looked freezing cold out there. There weren't going to be any serious swaths of tourists until the following summer. If Cadence was going to make money from her business, she'd better get creative and fast. Anyway, money from an upcoming event could help tide Darla over, too. Then again, Darla wouldn't need much help if she was going to move in with Cadence after all.

"What do you think, Tate?"

"About a winter event? Well, the first thing that comes to mind in the winter for me—in terms of merrymaking—is ice-skating. And there is a pond just south of here, about half a mile. It's inland in the woods. I'm sure it's frozen or close to it. A tiny thing. But if you don't want to be outside—and who could blame you—then the next bet is a Christmas party, but people generally like to be with family for Christmas, so that makes less sense, too, unless a family needs a venue for their Christmas party—but then, you don't have one of those unless—"

"Unless you and Darla move in with me." Cadence smirked.

"You don't like my animals," Tatum shot back.

Cadence replied, "Wrong. I *love* your animals, but I love my white carpets, too."

"Well, it's an impasse."

"Everything feels like it's at an impasse." Cadence sighed deeply.

Tatum looked thoughtfully at her. "Wait a minute. I think I have an idea."

CHAPTER 15—DARLA

Tatum's idea was simple: accept Cadence's offer to move in. As for the pets? They could go to work with her every day, saving the white carpets and Cadence's sanity, not to mention any potential conflict that could arise between the animals and the boys.

Since Darla wanted to resume her duties as director of the Nativity play, and since she really did need help, she accepted the idea. Reluctantly, but she accepted it. Her main gripe was that the number of moves she'd been through in the past ten months or so was getting a little out of hand. Regardless, it *did* make sense. All three of the girls were gone, and rooms sat empty in Cadence's house. Plus, if Tatum's idea was sincere, then this was a good transition. Especially before the boys got too settled.

But moving back into Cadence's house was going to require help. Someone had to be on baby duty. Someone had to be on animal duty. Someone had to break down and move furniture. The first two tasks were accounted for. Darla had the babies. Tatum had the animals—she'd take them out to the shelter and keep them segregated from the kittens and their mother. Cadence could do some of the heavy lifting, but she probably couldn't handle the cribs alone. It'd be nice to have a man around, which was why when Cadence suggested Rip, Hendrik's brother, Darla had jumped on the idea.

But Tatum turned it down. "We don't know him."

"I know him," Cadence argued as they sipped coffee Tuesday morning, mapping out the big move.

"Tate, I want this done soon. That way I can get to the school for Thursday's dress rehearsal."

Tatum glared. "How much do you know about Rip, though? Did he fight for some of Hendrik's money when he died?"

Cadence glared right back. "No. There was no money to fight for. And in fact, Rip actually paid for the funeral. All of it. The wake, the service, the burial...the coffin, the headstone, *everything*. What's your problem with Rip?"

"Nothing," Tatum grumbled.

"There is another option," Darla said. She didn't want to call him, and yet she was desperate to call him. She just hadn't had good reason to. And was asking for a favor really a good reason? Half their relationship seemed to be asking Mason Acton for favors.

But she'd already set it in motion. "Mason. *Of course!*" Cadence texted away furiously on her phone. Darla's stomach lurched at the possibility that she was texting Mason. Did she have his number?

She backpedaled right then. "He's probably teaching right now. Birch High doesn't get out until at least 3:30. Maybe later. But I mean, maybe he can check his phone during passing period? Or—" Darla found herself scraping away any excuse not to involve Mason in this whole matter despite logic and reason and... "I mean, maybe that's crazy. He's probably so tired at the end of the day." She willed Cadence to drop her phone, then pinned her younger sister with a hard look. "Tatum, why not Rip?"

"Rip's busy today anyway." Cadence flashed her phone.

Darla let out a breath on two accounts. One, that Cadence had been contacting Rip, not Mason. And two...that Rip wasn't an option. At least not right away.

"I'll ask Rip if he can come Thursday and Friday. Anything would help, right?"

"Not Friday," Tatum snapped. "I've got workers coming to the property then. And maybe Thursday, too, if my electrician contact can get out there. And I'm not sure I can take the animals with me. It'll be chaos. It's just...it's up in the sky right now."

"Up in the air," Darla corrected as a matter of habit. "I guess...Mason is our best bet?"

As luck would have it, Mason could come the day after tomorrow. Wednesday, after school. And doubly lucky, he had a boat—that didn't belong to his buddy Rip. All of this immediately piqued Darla's interest, and even her sisters seemed wildly curious about the changes in his life. But Darla dared not act too engaged in Mason's world.

Distance was best.

Distance was absolutely best. She would bet ten to one he agreed. *And* she would bet *twenty* to one he'd agree even more vehemently when he learned that Darla had not had just one baby...but two.

Fortunately for Darla, she had one full day to prepare for her reunion with the man she'd met just the summer before. The man who could have had her heart...under different circumstances.

CHAPTER 16—CADENCE

Wednesday morning, Cadence woke up to the smell of woodsmoke and chocolate. With no one else in the house yet, this made little sense. But her sisters had a key to the place, and so she wasn't surprised when she crept out into the living room to see a fire sizzling in the brick fireplace. It couldn't be considered a roaring fire by any stretch, but three neatly arranged logs burned red while chunky embers slowly detached and fell away. The heavy, earthen smell overwhelmed Cadence. It smelled painfully, heartachingly familiar.

It smelled like Hendrik.

But something other than Cadence's late husband was missing from the scene. What her sisters—or whoever was here—didn't know, was that Hendrik and Cadence didn't put on the first fire of the season until they had erected their Christmas tree, a task normally reserved for the day after Thanksgiving. A task that Cadence hadn't really wanted to give much attention to this particular year. Or maybe not ever again.

She staved off the urge to snap at Darla or Tatum as soon as one of them materialized, but then the scent of chocolate hit her once again, compounding on the heavy home scents. Cadence loved chocolate, and even in the wake of Hendrik's death, she'd enjoyed a Snickers or KitKat here or there. But *Christmas* chocolate—dark bars of bark laced through with peppermint and flecks of mistletoe red—what was the point? Such a romantic, delectable treat couldn't be enjoyed even a year or more on. It simply couldn't. She never wanted to eat Christmas chocolate or make hot cocoa or put up a Christmas tree again. Not without Hendrik.

And yet here she was, following the heady aroma like a cartoon teenager following a floating trail of bacon scent into his mother's kitchen.

There, at the stove with Angus the overgrown mutt at her feet, stood Tatum. Clad in pajamas and Hendrik's old apron—Kiss the Cook, it read—she was talking to herself and making nothing short of a grand-scale mess.

"What are you doing?" Cadence's breath turned shallow. Anger bloomed as red splotches up her neck. She could *feel* it.

Tatum, none the wiser, turned and grinned. She held a wooden ladle, and with it she stirred a pot of boiling milk while also scooping in spoons of dark chocolate bark crumbles—a box from the Christmas before. A box Cadence had intended to save for a special occasion. *This* was not a special occasion. And it wasn't meant for last-minute hot cocoa. Neither was the last bit of skim milk Cadence planned for her oatmeal. "I'm making hot cocoa."

"I can see that." Cadence seethed so hard she began to shake. "That's my chocolate bark."

"This?" Tatum shook the box, and it was then that Cadence's eyes swept the kitchen to see that two other mugs were already filled to the brim with this pseudo-holiday concoction.

"Stop." Cadence's nostrils flared. Her heart pounded in her ears. The skin on her neck burned. "*Now*."

Tatum froze, the box with its dregs still lifted. "O*kayy*."

This was no time for attitude. Cadence seized the

box, twisted the knob on the stove, and splashed scalding milk into the sink. Some jumped out and landed on her cheek, but her face was so hot, she barely noticed. "Get. Out."

"Cadence, calm *down*."

"Don't you dare tell me to calm down."

"But...what's the matter? We're moving in here. I can't make hot chocolate?" Tatum glowered back at Cadence, and the normally bubbly girl solidified into something different. Defensive. Older. "Cadence, what's wrong?"

Everything was wrong. Tatum never arose this early, for one. She never whipped up a special treat in the kitchen, for two. And she'd *definitely* never taken it upon herself to drag firewood in from the back deck and get a fire started, no matter how pathetic.

But mainly, it reeked of Hendrik. All of it. From the fire to the cocoa to the early morning surprise. Almost as if...as if Cadence half expected to find *him* in there, rather than her obnoxious little sister. Her breath came in pants, and nausea roiled in her belly. "I...can't..." She let her eyes flutter closed and gripped the edge of the counter. "I...can't *breathe*. I'm...*sick*... I'm—"

"Cadence!"

CHAPTER 17—TATUM

Tatum had never seen someone faint before.

Assuming that's what Cadence just did, there in the kitchen, sliding right down onto the washed-out wood flooring, one foot slipping beneath the beige shag rug like it could be a blanket and this whole thing was a strange little morning dream.

But it wasn't a dream, and Tatum had to act fast. Did she call 9-1-1? She dropped to the floor but froze. Did she move Cadence? What if it was a spinal problem? Tatum fumbled in the pockets of her flannel pajamas for her phone, praying it was even there, and her fingers shook as she tapped those three precious digits. But before she hit Dial, questions gripped her mind. She wasn't home in the city, just half a mile from the Northend fire station. She was on Heirloom Island, population in the hundreds, at *best*. If Tatum hit Dial, who would come? Tatum realized she didn't even know *if* there were emergency services on the island. Surely there must be. But the bill—weren't ambulance rides crazy expensive? What if the call directed Tatum to the mainland and they sent a patrol boat and—What would Cadence want her to do?

Then, as if it really *had* been a dream, Cadence's eyelids twitched. "Cadence!" Tatum forgot about the chance of paralysis and grabbed her sister's shoulders and shook.

Her body, at first as limp and mushy as Christmas pudding, turned rigid. Cadence's neck woke up first, lifting her head up off the floor in time for her eyes to crack open, then grow wide. "Huh?" she muttered, but it didn't quite sound like a *huh*. More like a grumble through a dry throat, her voice even cracking over the simple syllable.

"Cadence." Tatum searched her sister's face for some clue about her vitals. "What happened?"

"What?" Cadence twisted her head left and right and tried to sit up.

"No, wait. You, like, *collapsed*, Cadence. I almost called 9-1-1. Maybe I should still call."

At this, Cadence pushed Tatum's hand away and sat up straight. "No. Don't do that. I'm…" She squeezed her eyes shut and worked her jaw open and closed a few times. "I'm fine. I think I'm fine." But then her eyes fluttered again, and she heaved forward, clutching her stomach. "I feel like throwing up."

"We have to get you to a hospital. Something's wrong. Right?" Tatum didn't make a move despite her demand.

A faint knock drifted into Tatum's consciousness. Someone was at the door, but before Tatum could react to that particular disturbance, she heard the door open and Darla's voice break through the house, followed by the wail of a baby. "Cadence? Shep just wants to be rocked, but I'm *wiped*, can you—?"

"In here!" Tatum called out.

Cadence moved her body against the lower cupboards, her arms hugging her knees to her chest. Her head was between her knees, tucked into soft-looking pajama pants.

"Oh my gosh." Darla, who wore both boys in a twin carrier against her chest, gaped at Tatum.

"What happened?"

"I don't know," Tatum replied. "She, like, *fainted*. I don't know why. She says she might throw up." Tatum looked up at the babies, a fight-or-flight instinct taking over and giving her direction. "Stay back. Keep the babies back. In case it's contagious."

"Fainting spells aren't contagious." Darla shook her head and bounced the boys again to quiet Shepard, whose wails had turned to whimpers now.

"She needs to go in."

"In where?" Darla kept up the bouncing but took a step closer and spoke directly to Cadence. "Cadence, your doctor is on the island, right?"

Cadence shook her head but kept it down.

"Okay, there's an urgent care clinic on the island, right?"

Another shake of the head. Then, miserably, Cadence muttered, "Island doctor. Southeast side. Number on fridge."

Tatum whipped around to the fridge, finding a note with the name Dr. Gunther. She punched the numbers into the phone, only to get an answering service robo message. *Dr. Gunther is unavailable to take calls this week. If this is a medical emergency, please dial 9-1-1. If not, you can reach out to Dr. Gunther's associates in Birch Harbor.* Followed by a second phone number.

"Is this a medical emergency?" Tatum asked the others.

Darla looked alarmed. Cadence didn't react. "We need a boat to the mainland." She glanced at the clock. "Morning ferry leaves at 9. That's an hour away."

Darla shook her head. "No, we can't wait that long. She looks horrible."

"Thanks," Cadence grumbled, proving her emergency was less emergent, at least.

Darla let out a sigh. "Our boat is fixed. You'll have to drive her."

"I can't drive a boat!" Tatum shrieked.

"Neither can I," Darla returned.

"You've been out with Cadence like a million times, though."

"What about the babies?" Darla argued.

Tatum stood up from the floor and cinched the apron tie around her waist. "I'll watch them."

CHAPTER 18—DARLA

Leaving the babies with Tatum felt questionable, but what choice did they have? Schlep the babies on a boat to the mainland? It had already been a huge stressor just to bring them home. Newborns weren't supposed to ride boats.

What about a friend? Maybe a neighbor could take Cadence to the hospital? No, Darla was being ridiculous. She was the logical driver, and Tatum the logical babysitter. Besides, if Darla really and truly wanted to return to work right after Christmas, she'd better start testing out babysitters. Not that Tatum was a long-term solution...

Or was she?

Darla shelved the thought and took over fifteen minutes to coach Tatum on everything from feeding with the pumped milk to diaper changes to swaddling to screen time all the way to what Tatum ought to do in another emergency. This potentiality freaked all three of them out—even to the point that Cadence resisted going at all. "I'm *fine*," she growled once they'd gotten her bundled into a hat and scarf and her winter coat and boots. "If something happens to the babies, that's a *real* emergency."

"If something happens to the babies," Darla decided with finality, "Tatum is to call 9-1-1 and demand that Birch Harbor send a chopper. There's a helipad in the middle of the island just for this sort of thing. They don't fool around with boats when there are *actual* emergencies. Tatum." She held her sister's shoulders and spoke so crisply and clearly that Tatum would surely know that her main priority was babysitting. Not the shelter. Not Angus and the other pets who still needed to be fed breakfast. The babies came first. "Is that *crystal* clear?"

"Crystal," Tatum assured her.

THEY MADE it to the mainland in record time, and from there, to the hospital just outside of town. With her uneven breathing, Cadence was ushered right into triage and admitted directly, but her stay was relatively brief.

After two hours lying prone on the bed with saline bags and a heart rate monitor and blood pressure cuff and every other special medical accoutrement, Cadence asked Darla to see what the situation was.

After a brief hallway conversation with a nurse, Darla returned. "The doctor's on the way with results." She squeezed her sister's hand. "Just hang in there."

But the diagnosis that came half an hour later—without fanfare—was almost a letdown.

The MRI, the bloodwork, the X-ray, the readings—they were effectively conclusive. Cadence hadn't had a heart attack. Not a stroke. Not a seizure. No virus or respiratory issue or blood problem or anything.

The doctor stood at the foot of her bed, the heels of his hands pressed casually against the plastic bed frame. After listing off all the things Cadence didn't have, he gave a shrug. "It's good news."

"But what *was* it?" Darla asked, leaning forward in her plastic chair at Cadence's bedside.

The doctor straightened, folded his arms, and leaned back. "A panic attack." But his transition was quick. "We're going to give you medicine to help you relax. But that's short term, Mrs. Van Dam."

"A panic attack?" Cadence frowned and shook her head. "No. It was *real*. It was a physical thing. Not mental."

"Believe it or not, mental things can become physical things if we don't deal with them. Have you ever been treated for anxiety?"

Cadence scoffed. "No. Never."

"Many people suffer from some degree of it. That or even depression. They are in the same family of mental illness. Has anything happened lately that has you stressed? Maybe more than usual?"

Darla and Cadence looked at each other.

Darla answered for them both. "I just had twins, and Cadence is helping."

"That's stressful," the doctor confirmed. "Even if you're not the mother. Family often absorbs the stress—as well as the excitement—of a new baby." Darla felt this was a dig. As if the doctor were implying *she* should be the one in the hospital bed recovering from a panic attack. Little did he know she was nursing her own hardship. Maybe not full-blown postpartum depression, but certainly a degree of it. The difference between Cadence and Darla, however, was the future. Darla, despite her anxieties and fears and pure exhaustion, had something to look forward to: her dream had come true. She'd had her babies, and she had a job she loved, and she was living on a gorgeous island with her sisters. All in all, life was more than good for Darla. It was *great*. So then, why couldn't Cadence be happy, too?

"It's not just that," Darla interrupted, taking it upon herself to speak up on behalf of her broken sister.

"Not just the new family members?" he asked.

Cadence looked at Darla with interest, but also with a warning glint in her eye.

Darla went on. "We lost our father about a year ago."

"I'm terribly sorry," the doctor began, but Darla wasn't finished.

She gave her sister a warm squeeze and a smile, then said, "Cadence lost her husband around the same time."

The doctor looked at Cadence, not with a second

dose of sympathy, but instead with accusatory narrowed eyes. "Have you gotten help?"

"Help? My sisters are moving in with me. And I'm going to help at home with the babies. We help each other."

"I mean professional help."

CHAPTER 19—TATUM

It wasn't long after her sisters left that an urgent email appeared in Tatum's inbox. Not one to take her phone out to kill time, Tatum had grabbed it only to look up when to stop feeding a baby—if at all. She'd forgotten what Darla had said nearly the moment Darla had said it. Would Baby Gabriel know when he'd had enough? Or was it upon Tatum to ration his pumped milk?

The email popped up with a captivating subject line, irresistible to the likes of Tatum, who'd effectively propped each baby with his bottle in opposing nooks of the armchair. One slight movement, though, and the dominoes would fall and the perfect peace would be over.

She murmured the words to herself. "URGENT

HELP NEEDED WITH STRAY DOG." Then she opened the message to see the saddest picture of the sweetest little golden-colored puppy she'd ever seen, shivering on a thicket of fallen leaves in a corner behind the Koken—if the written contents were to be believed. Snow lapped at her paws, and her face strained from cold and hunger. Tatum couldn't believe that she lived in a time when precious pets like this one found themselves homeless and without food or drink. It crushed her soul, but then —that's exactly why she was doing what she was doing, wasn't it?

The man who sent the email—the owner of the Koken, apparently—went on to say he'd heard about Tatum's new undertaking through the grapevine. He had planned to send the dog off to the county pound on the next ferry but figured he'd get in touch first. This was great—it would be her second intake, and it'd really get her some attention. The only problem was that she was otherwise occupied right now, and with far more important matters.

She left her inbox and dialed up the Koken, asking to speak directly to Mr. Van der Sled. He came on the line, relief filling his thick Dutch-accented voice.

"Miss Sageberry, so glad you can help," he

started after she'd only just greeted him. "I have put dog in my truck with windows cracked, but snow is in forecast for this day, and I can't have cab fill up with snow. Ferry leaves soon. Can you come now?"

"Mr. Van der Sled, I'm so sorry. I can't get over there right now, but if you can just keep him until this afternoon—"

"No, *no*. I cannot!" He raised his voice, but Tatum sensed his frustration wasn't directed at her or the dog, but rather the fact that running a restaurant was a very stressful thing, indeed. "Dog must go. Lunch rush coming soon, and snow. Dog must go. Miss Sageberry, please?"

Tatum looked at the boys. Each had lost his little propped-up bottle and was sleeping soundly in his respective crook. They were so peaceful, she couldn't move them even if Darla had given her permission to take them somewhere, which Darla had not. In fact, Darla had distinctly said *no going anywhere*. Maybe the county pound wasn't so bad. Maybe the sweet island stray would be fine.

Maybe not.

Tatum chewed her lip, and Mr. Van der Sled huffed on the other end. "Hello?"

"Mr. Van der Sled," she said, cool, calm, and collected, "can you give me one hour?"

"One *hour*?"

"Just one hour. I can have someone there to get the dog and transfer her to our facility in one hour if you can keep her that long."

He huffed and grunted again. "Sure, sure, sure. Fine. But as soon as snow comes, I must let her out of truck. What if she must use toilet? On new upholstery, too?" He was getting worked up, so Tatum again promised him one hour, then hung up.

The only problem was, she didn't know a single soul on Heirloom Island who could transfer that doll of a dog. She herself could not do it. Her sisters were gone. She had no one else to help. Her Bait Shop colleagues were at work, after all. And that was the sum total of her contacts in these parts.

Unless...

Tatum snapped her fingers, then went to Cadence's fridge, searching for the same pinned note that had held the doctor's number.

Sure enough, there it was, the third number down after the dentist.

Mason Acton.

She called him, but it went to voice mail. Just as she was leaving a message, she realized *why* he couldn't answer: he was at work.

Instead of a voice mail, she switched to texting

him, explaining it was Darla's little sister and there was a situation wherein she needed help. She knew he was probably busy, but did he have any contacts on Heirloom Island? Or maybe one of his Hannigan cousins could ride over—wasn't Kate just across the lake at that adorable bed-and-breakfast? She had a partner or husband who had a boat—Tatum distinctly remembered this.

He replied a minute later, but that minute felt like a hundred minutes now that the clock was ticking at Mr. Van der Sled's Koken restaurant.

Sure do know someone. He can be anywhere on the island in ten minutes flat. Where should I send him?

Ten minutes flat could work. Way faster than she might have hoped for even if it were just Mason.

Should she have the guy go to the Koken directly? Then bring the dog down to the farm? But then, he wouldn't have a vehicle if he were coming from the mainland. It was best for him to get the dog and head directly to the shelter to avoid chaos at the boardwalk house, where the twins were. He could take a cab from the marina. Even in the dead of winter, there were often a couple of cabbies loitering for an easy fare.

Then another concern occurred to Tatum.

Would this plan bother Darla? Inviting a

stranger to where the babies were? It felt like a bad idea.

Tatum was good at bad ideas, and so she knew that whatever idea she had was probably the wrong one. She gave it another moment's thought before coming up with an inconvenient but hopefully safe option.

Please send him to the Koken to get the dog. Can he get a cab from there do you think?

Mason responded immediately.

He's on the island now. Works on the east coast.

Too perfect, she realized.

Okay, from there, have him come to the boardwalk. I will leave a key to my new property beneath the third potted plant on the third lakefront deck. He should take that key south along Continental Coast. Left at the last street on the left, Pine Beach Way. First driveway on the right. If he takes it, he won't miss the red farmhouse. Take the dog into the back barn and close the door. I'll be by as soon as I can, but he doesn't have to wait if he can't.

Tatum realized the extent of the favor she was asking before it occurred to her to inquire about who it was that Mason would enlist. Before she could ask, but after she'd gotten his confirmation, Shepard woke up wailing, and the rest of the morning fell into pure chaos.

Without so much as a chance to think about the abandoned dog at the Koken and her own pets next door and the kittens down the coast in the little farm, the morning flew by. It seemed like something erupted every five minutes. If not a crying baby, then a full diaper, and if not a full diaper, then a spit-up. By lunchtime, Tatum was finally getting a sense of the boys' routine. They wouldn't spit up unless they ate, and they weren't slated to eat for another thirty minutes at least, and this meant their diaper changes would come a bit later, too. Then, just as she got them back to sleep for what had to be their third catnap of the morning, the front door creaked open.

Tatum winced at the slight sound and froze near the playpen where both boys slept on either side of a mesh divider. Gabriel twitched, but his eyes remained shut. Shepard's eyes fluttered, but his body lay still. She slowly let out the breath she'd been holding in time to see Darla and Cadence emerge from the front hall.

Gesturing for them to meet her quietly in the kitchen, Tatum all but tiptoed that way, her entire body a mass of knotted muscles and frazzled nerves.

"This mom stuff is very hard," she hissed to Darla. "But they're great. Everything went well."

Then she looked at Cadence. "How are you? What's the prognosis?"

"You mean *diagnosis*?" Cadence looked fine, even bored, if a little tired. "A big, fat *nothing*, that's what." She kept her voice low, but Tatum still held her hands out and pushed air down with them as if to lower the volume even further.

"What do you mean *nothing*?" she whispered back.

Darla rolled her eyes. "It's not nothing. It was a panic attack, that's what. And those can be as serious as heart attacks—or at least, they can lead to heart attacks. Do you know that some people have literally died of broken hearts? It's a form of cardiomyopathy. And if Cadence doesn't take her diagnosis *as well as* her prognosis seriously, then she could be in for more attacks. Panic ones and heart ones."

Tatum squinted through the ocean of information. "Wait, so, do you have heart disease?"

Cadence waved her off, but Darla answered. "In a way, yes. She has depression. Maybe even post-traumatic stress disorder. Her grief." She smiled softly at Cadence and squeezed her shoulder, then looked at Tatum. "I don't think we've realized just how much Cadence is struggling. I don't think

Cadence has realized just how much she's struggling."

Tatum frowned, saddened for Cadence and disappointed in herself—and maybe Darla, too—for not realizing. "Cadence, I'm…I'm so sorry." She stepped up to Cadence and wrapped her in a hug. "I didn't—there's no excuse. I'm *sorry*."

"It's okay!" Cadence said too brightly, her voice funny and maybe phony. "Because I'm going to get *professional* help!" She drew her fist around her chest in a *hurrah* motion, and her tone was slick with sarcasm.

"Cadence," Darla chided firmly before looking at Tatum to explain. "The ER physician referred her for therapy. Cadence is just *thrilled*."

Tatum had never been good at sarcasm—using it or reading it—but she almost envied her sisters' application of it now. It was clear her helping days weren't over yet, not when it came to Cadence *or* Darla and the babies. But she did need to get to the shelter and see after that little yellow pup. "So…are you okay, then?" she asked cautiously.

"I'm embarrassingly fine, really." Cadence eased onto a barstool at the kitchen island, and she seemed to be moving quickly toward some form of acceptance of her fate. Tatum easily empathized with her. After all, all three of them had lost their dad. All three of them knew grief—like a dark friend, an unwelcome visitor. The difference, however, between Tatum and Cadence and maybe even Darla was her ability to cope. Tatum didn't have many abilities. Yes, she was patient with animals, and yes, she was easygoing and free-spirited, but those weren't skills, they were attributes. But boy could she cope. She could cope with quiet meditation and jovial celebration, with tears that came and went as easy as a PB sandwich. She could cope with remembering and laughing and all those sad thoughts flitted away like monarch butterflies with their orange dots of symmetry, fluttering up into the ether, sure to come back at some point but Tatum could let them go. Let them be.

Cadence, maybe, could not. She clung to grief, maybe. Toiled in it, even. And while Tatum would have expected this from Darla, what with the hormones and lifestyle overhaul, it wasn't unexpected from Cadence, either. They were more sensitive, her older sisters. More sensitive and more serious and more grounded. Tatum would rather be flying.

Darla set about making a fresh pot of coffee.

"You're going to see a therapist, then?"

"I guess," Cadence murmured; although, by now, they'd returned their voices to a normal volume, and the boys hadn't yet made a peep. After she got the coffee brewing, Darla left to check them.

"Good." Tatum nodded. "That's good." And if Cadence was good to go, with a plan and everything, then maybe Tatum could leave now? She asked as much once Darla had returned. "I had a new intake delivered to the property earlier today. Don't worry! I stayed here. It was sort of a coordinated effort. *Anyway*, am I okay to go handle that? And take my pups out and all?"

Darla and Cadence agreed readily that Tatum could go. As she went to leave, though, Tatum felt a surge of goodwill and generosity. "And Cade, whenever you need to go back into town to see your therapist, I can take you. I'll learn how to drive the boat."

"Actually," Darla replied, "she's seeing a therapist who's local, if you can believe that. He lives right here—works out of his house. *But*," she added emphatically, "it just so happens that her first appointment is Friday, the same day the boys have their two-week checkup in the morning here on the island with Dr. Brierson; then I'm going to bring them home and head back to the mainland for my two-week post-op checkup."

"Oh. Can you change it?" Tatum asked obtusely, wrapping herself in the scarf and blanket she'd worn over early that morning when she'd gone out on a limb and come to set up the hot cocoa.

Darla laughed derisively. "No, Tate. I was hoping you could watch the boys again."

CHAPTER 20—TATUM

Tatum checked on the dogs and Charm first. Angus was getting whiney. He was a big ol' lover, and he really needed human attention to thrive, so Tatum brought him along to the farm that day. Anyway, it wouldn't hurt to have a part-sheepdog, part-mastiff, part-whatever-in-the-world-Angus-really-was on hand. Who knew if Mason's so-called *contact* was a savory character? It'd behoove Tatum to take precautions. Anyway, it was highly unlikely the guy had stuck around at all. Who'd wait on a stranger like that?

In fact, who'd do a favor for a stranger like that? Maybe Mason had some really good islander friends that the Sageberrys didn't know about.

She came upon the front gate—which she'd

fixed up herself with twine, mainly—ajar. The snow was coming down heavily now, and the winding drive up to the farmhouse was sheeted over in white. She shifted into low gear and crunched up, and about halfway there, noticed another truck, Christmas-tree green, sitting near the lean-to that Tatum had begun to use for a carport.

The truck alone was no wonder. The guy—or girl?—was still here. What was a wonder, though, was the smoke curling out of the main chimney of the housetop. He'd put a fire on? *Why?* Now she was irritated.

"Angus," Tatum commanded, "heel." Angus leapt up to the front seat and sat sentinel as she unhooked his leash. Angus was as well trained as any purebred show dog—maybe even better trained than most. He'd mind her, leash or no leash. But if he had a leash on, it might only serve as an obstacle between saving his mistress's life or not. *Not* that Tatum felt threatened. But she did feel...*something*.

She popped open her driver's-side door and hopped into a fresh blanket of snow—which probably neared a foot deep by now, what with the new snow covering last week's fall. Angus joined her, falling onto his front two legs, then his back two in a graceful maneuver. She slammed the door shut and kept an eye on the house for movement. Briefly, Tatum imagined herself not as an animal rescuer, but rather as a policewoman investigating a small-time crime out in the snowy woods, all alone save her faithful and trusty companion. Almost like Starsky and Hutch or Holmes and Watson. Tatum wouldn't mind gnawing on an aromatic pipe, draped in a plaid tweed coat and wearing shiny black boots—as opposed to her thermal pajamas, which were currently bunched underneath a heavy down coat, ski pants she'd found at a thrift shop, and her sister's snow boots.

No movement appeared in the windows or at the door or over near the barn, so Tatum and Angus proceeded with caution. Angus sensed that she was on high alert, and as such, he stayed tight to her side, kicking up snow right along with her as they made their way to the farmhouse first; Tatum wanted to be sure it was just the chimney and not a full-on house fire.

They came upon the front door, its peeling white paint disguised by a layer of frost that had blown up across its broadside. Tatum had previously shaken out a threadbare rug she'd found wadded up in the corner of the porch, and it now, too, was iced over with snow and frost, but Tatum still stomped her boots hard, partly to clear them and partly to announce her presence. She leaned into the door, trying hard to decipher her and Angus's creaks from any that may be coming from within.

Soon enough, a clearly distinguishable sound *did* become audible. Even more than the sound itself was Angus's shift in posture. The hair along his spine settled and he dropped his barrel chest low, wiggling his rear and wagging his tail down into the accumulated snow.

Next came the noise—a panting, scratching noise just on the other side of the door. Tatum squinted at it, then at Angus, but the door flew open before she could turn the knob herself.

"Oh!" she said, startled. She flew into an unnecessary apology, then a rush of thank-yous as Angus tumbled through the door and exchanged sniffs and licks with the sweet little golden-hued mutt. It wasn't until the man's voice came in reply that Tatum even looked at him. This gave her a start all over again. "Oh!"

Standing there, his hands demurely tucked into his jeans pockets, looking taller than she remembered—and fitter, too—was none other than Rip Van Dam.

CHAPTER 21—CADENCE

As soon as Tatum left, Cadence felt pulled to take care of the babies. "You need a nap today, Darla. You came over here to get help this morning, then you ended up schlepping me to the mainland and spending the better part of the day sitting in a hospital room."

"Actually," Darla said through a telling yawn, "I am tired, but I feel *good*. I think getting out of the house was a breath of fresh air. Distracted me from the move."

"Right. Speaking of which, we really need to get a plan in place for tomorrow afternoon. Who's sleeping where *exactly*. Maybe you could do that thing you do in the theater with tape? To demarcate where things will go?"

Darla answered, swaddling Gabriel and then Shepard in a swift, proficient way before scooping them onto the armchair where she then deftly snuggled one into each arm and threw her head back. "This might be heaven."

Cadence looked at her. Darla glowed. She was meant for motherhood despite her fears and how much she was trying to run away from it all. Which, it was plainly obvious, was exactly what she'd be doing—trying to run away, run back to school and back to her job in the face of this major life change. Cadence wanted to broach this topic, she really did, but she also wanted to respect Darla's feelings and how hard her transition was.

Maybe discussing the move could trigger the right easement into the topic of Darla's fears and her impulse to run back to work, to run to the store, to run to Cadence's doctor's appointments and then her own.

"You look happier than I've seen you." Cadence heard the suggestion in her voice, and she sounded like a nagging mother. She hated that, but then again, she felt sincerely that it was her duty to help in every last way. Helping Darla would help Cadence, and clearly Cadence needed helping. She needed Darla and the boys.

She needed them to need her.

"Well, I'm happier than when I was pregnant, no doubt. Pregnancy was like a nine-month-long flu. I was achy and restless and nauseous and just *bleh*." She was taking it well. "But"—Darla flashed her eyes up at Cadence—"today *does* feel different. I don't know why. I guess—with Tatum babysitting, you know? It gave me some sense of freedom, like, okay, I can go out for a little while and come home to, well"—she smiled and looked down at the boys—"*this*. Guess I just needed a little break."

"Breaks are good."

"They are good," Darla agreed. "You need to take one, too, Cadence."

Cadence scoffed. "I am. I'm not at work. I want to stay here and be with you and the babies. That's a break for me."

"Okay, maybe it's not a break you need, then."

"Who says I need anything?" Cadence grew defensive. She was totally fine. She was over-the-moon happy and *better* than fine, actually. Life was perfect. The only thing that would make any of this better was Hendrik, but that wasn't a reality, and so—

"You're thinking about Hendrik." Darla said it flatly but not cruelly.

Cadence shrugged. "Of course. I always am."

"It's okay to move on, you know."

"I am moving on. I'm moving on with you and Tatum, the boys. And my new events business, too."

"Do you have any events planned?"

This was beginning to feel like twenty questions, and Cadence wasn't one for road-trip games. "Well, I found tenants for your place, actually—I forgot to mention it. Rip's construction team needed lodging. The motel on the north shore was nearly booked, so we struck a deal."

"Wait a minute," Darla cautioned her. "You already rented out our place? Cadence, you were going to host something there."

Cadence felt tense again, but not like the panic attack from that morning. Not that tense. Just… mainly…sore. Tired. From arguing and defending her actions. "I didn't want to lose income. It fell into my lap last night. Actually, it wasn't even Rip who reached out, it was a secretary for his company. I guess she found one of my old listings for the first house and wanted to see if it'd come open yet. It's just a six-month arrangement."

Darla seemed to consider this. "Well, it's good to have that income."

"Exactly. I don't even need to have any events

planned now. I'm set. I could quit teaching if I wanted."

"But do you want to?"

"I mean..."

"Cadence, *seriously*? You love teaching. It's your vocation. I mean, you love the church, and the church is the school, and it's taken the place of—"

"Of Hendrik? You think something needs to take his place?" Cadence felt her eyes get watery, but she knew it was the exhaustion, not true emotion. Her tears had long since run dry when it came to her late husband. She was sure of it. "Nothing can take my husband's place—and no one. Not a job, not another man, not a hobby or a new business—not even *you*." She froze. It was too far. She'd gone too far.

Darla's face turned to ice. "Well, that's good. Because I have no intention of taking anyone's place. And neither does Tatum. And neither will my children. We aren't here to fill some hole in your life, Cadence. We're here to be together, as family. Whatever else happens, *fine*. But we aren't some second-string group of understudies waiting for our chance to be the center of your world."

Angry with herself and with the world, Cadence turned to go, making it as far as the staircase, which she planned to climb until it took her all the way up to heaven to be with her first-string. Her lead. Her *Hendrik*. Who never would have said such ugly things to her. *Never*. Tears stung her cheeks and her throat closed up with the threat of a full-blown sob just as she started her ascent.

But sisters never did know when to quit, and Darla added loudly, "And don't forget to call that therapist to confirm your appointment!"

CHAPTER 22—TATUM

"Rip?"

"Hiya, Tatum. I, ah..." He scratched the dark stubble along his jaw. "Mason said you needed help, and I had the time." He returned his hand to his pocket and shrugged, his mouth forming a lopsided smile.

Tatum wasn't quite sure how to respond. In her brain, Rip was irritating. Too nice and too helpful, but on the whole, generally irrelevant to her own life. Rip was her sister's uninvolved, borderline-estranged brother-in-law. Young and foolish, and not a *thing* like Hendrik. Family lore had it that Rip had family money he wouldn't spare for his brother's medical bills. Family lore also had it that Rip barely managed to attend the funeral, he was so out of the picture. Family lore had a lot to say about baby-of-the-family Rip.

But in her chest and her throat and at the valley of her belly, Rip was none of that. He was...Tatum couldn't put her finger on it, actually.

"Thank you," she said at last, remaining on the doormat and now shivering, although she wasn't cold. Not by a mile. She actually felt quite warm. Flushed, even.

But he stepped to the side in an awkward shuffle and held his arm inward. "Here, come on in. I've got the woodstove going. The furnace isn't working, I s'pose. But if you keep the stove running, it's tolerable in the kitchen, at the very least. I see that's where you've got a little cat family. I've got the kitchen door closed so they don't mingle. Although, this little girl seems easy as apple pie when it comes to new friends." His rambling gave way as he lowered to the ground and scrubbed both dogs at once. Their affectionate attention turned to him, and they lapped at his face and neck and hands. He didn't mind a single slobbery second of it.

Tatum dropped down, too, assessing the new pooch, who regarded her with more caution than she regarded Rip. This made sense, since Rip had been there with her for some hours now.

"Hey girl," Tatum cooed as she felt her paws—rough—and behind her ears—matted. "Poor thing. She needs a bath and brush. Maybe a trim."

"I looked around for supplies, but—what exactly is this place, anyway?" Rip scratched his head, and Tatum wondered if he was going for a cartoon effect, because that's just how he looked. She forced down her smile.

"I'm opening an animal shelter here," she answered, looking around at the near-empty parlor. This room alone proved just how old the property was. Other than peeling, dated wallpaper, it boasted scuffed and soggy hardwood floors that once must have gleamed with a fresh, waxen glow. The chair rail was missing in chunks at various points, but its dark wood perfectly matched the hearth of the modest fireplace. The spread of floor in front of the fireplace was darkened with soot—as was the brick that rose up away from the dark, ashy fireplace chamber. Left over in this front parlor room was a once-ornate sofa, upholstered in a style not unlike what Tatum imagined people of the French countryside to prefer, with pink-petaled flowers and ropey vines and a sweet curve to the back and arms of the piece.

She noticed now that there was a fresh set of firewood in the fireplace and that the screens were pushed open.

Rip must have seen her take notice because he said, "I tried to hold off on starting a second fire in here. Didn't want to waste your wood, but even if I did, I'd have cut you more. I own a whole lot on the east coast, and we're turning half into lumber."

"A lot?" She lifted an eyebrow. "Is that another Van Dam family heirloom?"

"Naw. Just mine." He answered simply, his eyes steady on Angus, whose belly he was scrubbing.

"Ah, so that's why you were here. This morning, I mean. Mason said you were already on the island." She tried to state all of this as pure fact so that he would take the hint and go, but truth be told, she didn't want him to go. It'd be nice to have company. Plus—and maybe this was boredom—Tatum sort of wanted to know why he was on the island. Was he living on this lot now? Had he moved out of his house north of Birch Harbor? She gave her head a quick shake. Tatum hated being so curious about Rip. She had a lot to do today, and this small talk was wasting her time, really. Indeed, Tatum indicated toward the bedroom. "I'd better get to work. I have a lot to do."

"Do you need any help?" He half followed her

toward the bedroom. Inside of the closet in there was where she kept a box of basic animal grooming supplies and some snacks and bottles of water for herself.

In the bedroom, she'd also made up the iron-frame bed that had been left behind. It was silly to have a bedroom in the rescue, but Tatum figured it would be sillier to get rid of perfectly good furniture, and while she was working toward a grand opening, she might as well have a good napping spot.

"Help me? I don't really—well..." She turned at the bedroom door, suddenly uncomfortable and elated all at once. Never in Tatum's life had she had a serious boyfriend. Or even *any* boyfriend. She'd been on dates, sure. And she was becoming hot at the growing awareness that this silly little favor was starting to feel like a date even though it was *definitely* not a date. Obviously not. She was so ridiculous to even think it. And Rip was ridiculous to be following so closely behind her now. When she turned, she nearly turned into him, in fact. "I mean —" Now she felt bad. He looked so earnest. "Don't you have to get back? To wherever you were?" It occurred to her that she didn't know where he'd been or where he was going when Mason had called upon him to help.

She forced herself to move into the bedroom, ignoring the fact that she felt like a giggling, nervous teenager whose boyfriend was stopping by to pick her up and here they found themselves at the threshold of her bedroom, with her parents just in the next room, listening to make sure no funny business took place. She forced the thought out of her brain and grabbed a bottle of Mane 'n Tail shampoo and its corresponding jug of conditioner. Then she turned and looked at him, waiting politely for his answer.

"Actually, no, I don't have to get back." He brushed his hands down the thighs of his jeans. Tatum knew this because she couldn't seem to stop looking at him, at every inch of him—at his kind-but-rough hands and his snug jeans and Carhartt jacket and— "I'm heading up a project over that way. A charter school is going up."

Now even more interested, she passed him the bottles and threw him a suspicious look. "Are you the principal?"

He chuckled, then said definitively, "No. The contractor. My company won the bid to build the facilities for the first phase."

They started seamlessly working together, in tandem, as Tatum continued an inquiry into Rip's job and project. She set about boiling a kettle of water with an age-old cast-iron number—also left behind. He set a big galvanized basin on the kitchen floor after relocating the cat family slowly and carefully into the second bedroom—a spare room empty save for an old cracked secretary desk.

"I didn't know there was a new school going up on the island. Seems to me St. Mary's is barely able to keep open with its few students. Who'll go to the charter school?" It was as sincere a question as any, and Tatum didn't realize she sounded defensive.

But Rip's reply came softly while they both worked warm suds into the stray's overgrown coat. "I guess kids who aren't Catholic." He was frank in his delivery, but Tatum still didn't understand.

"You don't have to be Catholic to go to St. Mary's."

"Right, well. What do I know? I'm just following the work."

This struck Tatum as funny. The sort of person who *just followed the work* had to be at odds with a sort of person like Tatum. Tatum, who never followed the work and who only followed her heart. The air shifted, and soon enough, the dog was washed, conditioned, and rinsed. Tatum pulled a towel down from a nearby chair and passed it to him. "I, um, need to go check on something."

"Oh, sure. I got the pooch. Don't worry." His voice twisted goofily into the sort a loving dad might use with his toddler daughter, and he held the dog's muzzle. "I got you, don't I, Miracle? Yes, I do. Yes, I sure *do*, you sweet lil' thing, you."

Tatum crossed her arms. "Miracle?"

He glanced at her, then looked again at the dog and gave her another rubdown with the towel. "Oops. She knows our secret, doesn't she?" The dog yipped playfully, then barked at Tatum, and suddenly it was two against one. Tatum wondered where the heck Angus was.

"What secret?" she asked, playing along with a skeptical gaze.

"I named her. I mean, you don't have to keep it or anything. I guess rescue dogs probably go through at least two names. Maybe more, depending on how they came to be rescues. You know, the name they come in with, the name the shelter gives them, and then the name they get in their furever home."

"You know about furever homes?" He was using her language, and it made Tatum feel funny.

"Sure. I rescued an old boy last year. Kept him comfortable until it was time. Benny. Sometimes I thought about getting a few others and just calling them *The Jets*. Get it?" He gave her a goofy grin, and there it was. That twist in Tatum's gut again.

"Yeah, I get it. But *Miracle*?"

"As in Christmas miracle, you know? I mean, it was a miracle she made it as long as she did out there in the freezing snow. She made it here, to you. I mean, to me, it's a Christmas miracle."

"Miracle." Tatum's heart throbbed. She loved it. All of it. The story, the name, the…well, just, all of it. "Yeah." She smiled at Rip. "I like that. *Miracle*."

CHAPTER 23—DARLA

Later that afternoon, Mason was due to help with the move, and Darla found herself stuck in her bedroom in the middle house, her makeup and hair products splayed across the counter in a mess of beauty supplies. She'd never been a disorganized person, only ever a careful, neat person. And normally, Darla kept her morning routine to the bare minimum. Pregnancy hadn't changed that, of course, but now that the boys were here, any morning routine Darla had ever enjoyed had gone out the window.

As she now selected a tube of concealer, it was as though she'd lost all muscle memory. Dabbing it beneath her eyes felt like an act of futility—as did the coat of mascara and the round brush and curling iron and—*sigh*. When she finished, she looked just as much the tired mom as she did when she began.

Tatum didn't have much; somehow, she'd managed to move over most of her clothes and personal effects. The furniture she wanted to take was tagged in sticky notes. She planned to leave and work at the farmhouse and return after three, when Mason was scheduled to arrive. That morning, particularly, Tatum had gotten up extra early, looking spry. She'd even washed her hair and dried it and applied a smudge of red lipstick. The last time Darla had seen Tatum do anything to her appearance was before they moved to the island. It was highly suspicious, in fact, but Darla was too busy worrying about her own looks, which really ought to be just as suspicious. She was two weeks postnatal; how could she possibly care about her looks in the face of a male acquaintance at a time like this? It was not only preposterous, but indecent, really. Just the idea that Darla was gussying herself up made her cringe with embarrassment and shrink from guilt. Shameful. Shame on her. With that, she wiped off the apricot lipstick she'd applied and mussed her hair, then slapped her hands on her growing saddlebags and turned from the mirror.

On cue, Gabriel began to fuss, and when one of

the babies so much as fussed, Darla could count on her body reacting accordingly. She hadn't yet learned to be prepared with nursing pads, and before she knew it, milk had soaked right through her shirt. She pulled off her sweater and bra and pulled out a spare nursing bra from her diaper bag. It was a fancy one that was especially uncomfortable—Tatum had bought it from a lingerie store, naturally. This was why Darla kept it in the bag—because so far, she hadn't needed to change out, and it made sense to save the uncomfortable, lacey nursing bra for emergencies. But right now, it'd have to do because everything was either packed or already in her new closet next door. Gabriel's fussing turned to cries, and Darla decided to feed him before going down to get a new top. Shepard was hungry, too, and by the time they wrapped up their afternoon snack, it was well past three. Tatum should be home.

But she wasn't yet. Darla had few remaining options—either wear the sweater with damp spots or hurry downstairs and pull something out of the last-minute box into which she'd thrown her cell charger, the book she was reading, last night's outfit, and her pajama T-shirt.

She rummaged through the box, settling on the T-shirt, which smelled fresh from her bath, but when she stood to pull it on, the door opened.

Darla screamed and held the thin fabric against her tummy, but she moved awkwardly and it left her cleavage protruding above. She felt her cheeks redden like beets as her eyes lifted to none other than the *last* person whom she would've liked to have see her two weeks after pregnancy and two *minutes* after nursing *two* babies.

"Mason."

He swiveled away from her, his hand raised to the back of his head while he mumbled something that sounded like an apology.

Darla was humiliated. It was she who ought to apologize. "I am *so* sorry. I wasn't thinking; I just needed to change my shirt. And—" She had the pajama tee on, but Mason was still turned away. "I'm *clothed* now," she finished weakly, walking backward toward the stairs so she could retreat into her bed and stay there for the rest of the afternoon until he'd left.

But Mason held his hand out to stop her. "No, no, no, please don't apologize. It was my fault. I should have knocked, but Tatum said to just come in."

"Tatum's home?"

"I saw her just outside. She and Rip. They pulled up in his truck, and I think she was going over to Cadence's house to get her pets situated or something." He pushed a hand through his hair, and Darla couldn't be sure, but she almost saw a ripple of muscle in his forearm, and it reminded her of a time that now felt ages away. A time when she had a crush on this sweet, helpful man with his rippling forearms and lush head of hair and deep voice and—*ugh*. She felt weird now. He'd basically seen her half-naked, or almost, and here he was rambling about Tatum and Rip, and— "Rip?" *Wait a minute*, Darla thought. "What's he doing here?"

"Oh, I figured you knew. He's been helping Tatum on her property. Yesterday and today, at least."

"That's good," Darla replied, now on the first step of the staircase. She needed to get back upstairs for her own dignity and more importantly, for the boys, who got restless easily. As if they knew when they weren't being supervised. "I've got to get upstairs. Again, I'm *really* sorry you had to see that just now." She bit her lower lip and retreated up another step, but Mason smirked, and the smirk turned into a lopsided smile, and the smile carried his gaze away from her and out the windows toward the lake.

However, just as she accepted that he was as embarrassed as her, and maybe even a bit horrified, he said, "Actually, um, I kind of liked it."

Darla felt her neck and chest grow hot, and she gaped at him, but he kept his eyes on the snowy view of the lake. "Sorry. Jeez. That was inappropriate."

She forced her jaw shut and opened it again to find the right response, but all she could manage was, well, the truth. "Actually, *I* kind of liked it."

His head snapped up, and he looked her right in the eyes. "Darla, I've really missed you."

Darla leveled her chin. She'd missed him, too. She'd ached for what they'd nearly had. All through her pregnancy, she'd ached. But these last two weeks —they'd changed things.

Hadn't they?

It wouldn't do to get his hopes up. It wouldn't do to get her own hopes up, either.

She had to break it to him, and she had to do that now before things got awkward while he helped move her and Tatum's furniture. "Mason, can we—" She blinked and felt the threat of a tear surface at the corner of one eye. "Maybe we can see each other again?"

His face lifted, and his body seemed to move toward the staircase, toward her, away from the rest of the world and the distance they'd cultivated, but she held up a hand. "I mean *as friends.*"

CHAPTER 24—TATUM

Having Rip around to help was proving more useful than Tatum could have predicted. Plus, he made her laugh. Plus, he was super-duper nice. Like, almost too nice. Nicest guy Tatum had ever known, in fact. And then, of course, there was the fact that he just *looked* different to her than the last time she'd seen him, which was at the summer reunion party he'd helped with.

Six months could change a person; Tatum knew this from her own experience and the experiences of her sisters, sure. But she could have sworn she recalled him being way less...well...*attractive*.

So, all these factors had meant Tatum's productivity sort of spiked. She got up earlier that morning.

Put on lipstick and fixed up her hair—or at least fixed it up as much as was possible. Tatum was a no-fuss kind of gal. A straight, almost-black shoulder-length bob with an even thatch of bangs could be quite the wash-n-wear hairdo. As for lipstick, she just had one tube of cranberry red, which Cadence had given her for Christmas over ten years before. That it went on so easily—and even sort of *stayed* on—felt as much a Christmas miracle as Rip's insistence that he adopt the golden mutt. He said he could be her first Furever Home Success Story, holding up his hands to frame the words like they were meant for a billboard.

Maybe the words—along with a picture of the charming Rip Van Dam and the spunky golden girl he'd named Miracle—really were meant for an ad. It was something Tatum could easily wrap her head around. It was as if she could visualize her dream more clearly than ever, and anything that got in the way of it could be surmountable. *Anything*. Almost.

But the contention that had started brewing between Cadence and Darla again might be the one thing that Tatum would not overcome. She couldn't live sanely in a house with two feuding sisters. Something would have to give, and fast, otherwise

Tatum had no problem spending even more time at her property.

After all, Rip had already offered to bring his HVAC guys over to install a new furnace at cost, and he planned to patch up the wall in the kitchen the very next day. Everything at the farmhouse was turning up daisies, and Tatum wasn't about to let Cadence and Darla ruin it for her.

Rip had offered to help Mason move some of the furniture pieces that evening, and the next day he'd come back to keep working on the farmhouse. His contracting duties were mainly supervisory, but the recent snowfall had stalled the project anyway. The whole situation was a little too perfect because before Tatum even knew it, Cadence had offered to rent the middle house to the crew. This surprised Tatum because it was distinctly *not* in Cadence's best interest—or Darla's—to support the planning of a whole new school. Tatum had even wondered if Cadence *knew* what Rip and his team were hired to build, but it wasn't her business to say. At least, not yet. Not until the dust had settled between the sisters anyway. One more conflict would only serve to escalate things, not fix them.

Rip and Mason linked up at the middle house, where they had just a few heavy pieces to bring over.

Meanwhile Tatum joined Cadence in Darla and the boys' new room, where she was hanging the mobile and resurrecting the little bookshelf with baby books. They first poured themselves some hot cocoa and set the fire—Cadence said she liked the fire now; it reminded her of Hendrik and maybe that wasn't a bad thing. She liked to be reminded of him, even after her *spell*, as she called it.

Tatum just went along with everything, but a question nagged at her, and she figured Cadence was the logical person to answer it.

Suddenly a little too warm, she pulled off her red sweater and tossed it across one of the cribs before falling to her knees at the little library. "Cadence," she began primly, assuming as serious an affect as she could.

"Yes?" Cadence of late had been a little *not herself*. Too mellow and too agreeable.

"Um, what happened to Rip?"

Cadence paused, a children's lift-the-flap Bible in her hand. "What do you mean?" Then she clicked her tongue. "Oh, you mean why's he on the island? I guess this new building project. I'm not sure exactly what it is. I haven't had a chance to ask him. But, yeah. I think things are going well for Rip these days." Then she shook her head. "I never would have taken him for a go-getter, though. Especially compared to Hendrik. I mean—" She pursed her lips and looked thoughtful. "They were total opposites. Rip lived at home until he was thirty, I think."

"How old is he now?" Tatum asked, distracted momentarily from her *actual* question, which Cadence had misinterpreted.

"I think he's Darla's age. Around thirty-five. Hendrik told me he was an afterthought baby. His parents had Rip when they were much, much older. I think his mom was nearly fifty. It was quite a shock for the family. That's why they weren't close—Rip and Hendrik. Rip was basically a baby cousin to him, and not much more. Plus he was a latchkey kid. He had the run of this island. Always in trouble, I guess."

"Well, that's not what I meant." Tatum busied herself by picking up a stack of board books and pretending to sort them alphabetically.

"Oh. What did you mean?"

"He looks different." Tatum felt herself flush, so she scratched a nonexistent itch on her cheek, shielding her face from Cadence.

"Different? Really?" Cadence clearly didn't notice Tatum's visceral reaction to even broaching this conversation.

"Yeah. I mean…like *better*."

That did the trick.

Cadence slotted the children's lift-the-flap Bible, then turned and looked at Tatum with new eyes. "*Better?*" She raised both eyebrows.

Tatum could not squash the smile spreading across her face. "I mean, yeah. Like…cuter or something."

"*Cuter?*" Cadence shook her head. "I don't think he looks any different than he ever has. Maybe he got a new haircut."

Tatum shook her head right back. "No. He's definitely different. Maybe he's in better shape or he got plastic surgery, or—"

Cadence belted out a laugh. "No. No, now I'm *sure* of it. Rip Van Dam looks the exact same. He hasn't changed. I mean—other than he's become way more responsible in the last couple of years, I guess. Or maybe the last few months." She frowned at Tatum, an amused sort of frown where her eyes sort of shimmered. "It isn't Rip who's changed."

Tatum recoiled in skepticism. "What?"

Cadence turned to her, grabbing both of Tatum's hands in hers and squeezing them with glee. "It's you. *You* have changed."

CHAPTER 25—CADENCE

Tatum acted totally nonchalant and even disbelieving in the face of Cadence's revelation. Cadence repeated herself. "Tatum, you've changed."

But Tatum just shook her head and acted suddenly very interested in sorting the baby books. "No. I haven't changed. Rip looks different. He probably just lost a few pounds or dyed his hair or—"

"You never thought he was cute before. When you saw him this summer, he, what? Aggravated you?"

"Exactly."

"So, what has changed since then?" Cadence asked rhetorically. "He's in motion with his contractor business. It did well after Hendrik passed because suddenly there was no more family pressure. You moved here for the long haul. Started working on your dream. He helped you. You both *look* the exact same as before."

"Maybe it's just magic or something."

Tatum was brushing the conversation aside, but Cadence knew better than to let her. Cadence loved Rip like family because he *was* family to her. But she wasn't about to let Tatum nurture a schoolgirl crush. Not when the object of her affection was the wildcard who was Rip, a party boy in his younger years and a mama's boy in his twenties. Cadence pushed off from the floor and brushed her hands on the tops of her thighs. She pursed her lips. "It's not magic. It's called growing up. But let me assure you of something, Tatum." She felt her *mom voice* growing heavy, but she couldn't help it; she had to be the mother in this particular situation. "Rip's the same screwball he always was."

She turned to go but found Darla in the doorway, the twins strapped to her chest in the baby carrier. Cadence blinked. "Oh. We were just finishing up in here. I'll be downstairs if you need me."

"Wait a minute," Darla said. "What are you talking about? What's magic—or not?"

Cadence glanced back at Tatum, who pouted on

the floor. She replied for both of them. "Tatum was wondering if Rip had changed. She thinks he's suddenly become attractive or something." She laughed—without mirth, though. "I just told her he's the same old goof he's always been." Cadence smiled. "I have to go. I've got my first appointment tomorrow morning, and I want everything done tonight so that I'm not overwhelmed in the morning."

"Your therapist appointment?" Darla pried.

Cadence pressed her mouth into a thin line. "Yep." She kept her tone short with Darla, but her eyes flickered to the boys. She couldn't resist. She leaned in and gave each a kiss on the head. "Think about what you two want to do for Christmas this year. I need to know if we're doing something together or if I'm just going to celebrate with the girls on the mainland."

"You're not going to stay here for Christmas?" Tatum protested.

Cadence flipped her hair over her shoulder. "I mean I'd love to, but I have the girls to think of as well. They may have other plans."

Darla scoffed. "They'll come here. Why wouldn't they? This is their home, right?"

Cadence just raised her eyebrows. "Well, now

that you two live here, there isn't much space for them anymore, is there?"

A cold feeling trickled up her spine, sending shivers through her entire body. Cadence knew what she was doing. She was behaving badly. Being cruel. But Darla had been cruel first, and everything felt hard and wrong and sad and terrible. Cadence's pain was just too great.

She'd messed up. She never should have opened her heart to her sisters again. She never should have brought them back into her house. She'd thought she could start fresh and have a new family. She could help with the boys, and she could help her two best friends in the world.

But as it turned out, they didn't need her.

CHAPTER 26—DARLA

Darla and Tatum looked at each other for a moment after Cadence left.

"Remember that one?" Darla said at length, pointing to the lift-the-flap Bible Tatum had just pulled from the middle shelf of the bookcase and propped open on top.

Tatum looked at the book, fondness gleaming in her gaze as Darla lowered to the rocking recliner facing Tatum and the shelf.

"I sure do. I always loved the story of Christmas. I mean, what kid didn't, you know?"

"I always thought it was a little sad, to tell you the truth," Darla replied.

Frowning, her sister plucked the book back and turned to the story, which was situated in the middle of the board book, complete with open-able stable doors, a manger, and wise men whose hands also opened, revealing each of the three precious gifts for the Little Lord Jesus, asleep on the hay.

Tatum concentrated on the simplified story and its accompanying images of Mary, Joseph, the newborn babe, a smattering of barnyard animals, and the twinkling night sky.

Darla explained, "I just think of how scared Mary had to have been to find herself pregnant like that. It had to be uncomfortable and frightening, and what about Joseph? Was she afraid he wouldn't support her? Then the journey through the desert and the night, walking to her virgin labor. She had no mother or sister there. Just this man she relied upon, and then lo and behold there was no room at the inn. To be turned away in that condition—" Darla physically shuddered. "I can't imagine. So she winds up in a barn, effectively, and there she gives birth to the world's Savior. *Wow*."

"But it's not sad," Tatum argued, more earnest now. "It's a message of hope for the world. And strength and excitement, too. It was the best thing to happen to the world, Baby Jesus's birth. How could that be sad?"

Darla considered this. "Maybe *sad* is the wrong

word. Maybe *somber* is better. You know? The story of Christmas is just so quiet, and it's so critical, too."

"It's a birthday story, though." Tatum looked utterly stumped, and Darla felt they were at polar ends of the spectrum of common understanding. Then she asked, "Did you think it was a sad story even when you were a little girl?"

Darla blinked. "No? I mean, I guess not. When I was little, I just saw it as, like, a companion story." She couldn't help but laugh a little at that. "You know, to Santa Claus."

"Right." Tatum smiled. "I guess I still believe in Santa Claus." Then she looked more seriously at Darla. "Is it sad because you've changed, maybe? You know, you had your babies, and now you can appreciate Mary's story in a different way."

Darla smiled at her little sister. "I think you're absolutely right. I think one's perception of a situation changes when one, herself, changes. Does that make sense?"

Tatum nodded eagerly. "That's what Cadence was trying to say, I think."

"Oh?"

"Yeah. I could have sworn Rip looked different to me yesterday when I met him at the farm. He just *does*, you know? Like he's changed somehow. But Cadence says he looks the same to her."

"He looks the same to me, too," Darla answered.

"So, it *is* me who's changed. But I have no idea why. It's like magic or something."

"You like him." Darla said this knowingly—as if it were a matter of fact. An eventuality that her little, spunky sister would fall for the youngest Van Dam. Even when Darla had met him that summer, she felt he reminded her somehow of Tatum.

But Tatum shook her head, her black bangs brushing like a curtain along the tops of her eyebrows. Sometimes, she really did look like a little girl, especially now. Especially to Darla, who herself was no longer a little girl, but rather a mother.

Darla sucked in a breath and rocked the boys back and forth. Cradling them against her in their carrier proved to be the most peaceful thing in the world. They loved it. She loved it. Like they weren't meant to have left her body—not quite yet. "Tatum, I think Cadence is right, but sometimes we aren't ready to see something in ourselves. And when we go through a change—when we become settled and happy and find whatever it is we're looking for—then the reality before us sets in. We see not just the good—like the story of Christmas—but the bad, too.

Or at least the *hard*." She was quiet a moment while Tatum looked thoughtful. "And the opposite is true. When we are happy, and we start to become our true selves, we see the good out there where maybe before we saw the bad."

"You're saying I am happy now, and so I can appreciate Rip more than when I was still…"

"Searching?"

"Yeah." A smile formed over Tatum's mouth. "We see the whole story for what it is. Not just what's maybe in ourselves." But her smile slipped away. "Does this mean one day that I'm going to think of Christmas as a sad time, too?"

Darla laughed. "*Sad* was maybe the wrong word. But anyway, you get to decide how you feel about things. Maybe one day, you'll see that the meaning of Christmas is less aligned with our childhood belief in Santa and—I don't know—more aligned with your own feelings about relationships and duty and burden."

"You're saying being a mother is a burden."

"Absolutely," Darla replied firmly. "Not in a bad way, but in an important way. It is a mother's burden to bring her children safely into the world. And Mary epitomized that. She journeyed, as just a girl, across miles to give birth to humanity's salvation. It was a blessing to her, but it was a burden. Of the highest and most critical order."

"All I know," Tatum replied, "is that those two are the sweetest little burdens I ever laid eyes on." She stood and crossed the room, bending to kiss each baby on his head.

"And they are my greatest blessings. Through these boys, I see the world differently."

Tatum's face went somber. "Through my animal rescue, I see the world differently."

Nodding, Darla grabbed her hand. "Listen, Cadence is in a hard place. Whatever she had to say about Rip—who he is and how you feel about him—you need to take with a grain of salt. She hasn't had her Christmas yet."

But Tatum looked more confused than ever. "What do you mean? She had Hendrik. He was her world."

Darla pressed her lips together and rocked the boys again, thinking how best to answer that. After a beat, she said, "Just like Christmas is a season of miracles, so, too, can there be other seasons of miracles. Maybe meeting Hendrik was her Christmas, but she still has Easter waiting."

CHAPTER 27—TATUM

Over the next day, Tatum thought hard about what her sisters had meant—both of them. Cadence with her wisdom about perspective and Darla with hers. Cadence remained moody and closed off, even as Tatum reminded everyone that she was going to babysit on Friday, that way each sister could go to her doctor's appointment.

Rip, yet again, promised to help. First, he needed to get his crew the key to their winter rental next door, but then he'd come over and hold the babies, feed them, change diapers if he had to. He was game for anything. Tatum liked that about him.

Just an hour into her morning with Gabriel and Shepard, the phone rang. It was Darla with an idea.

"I haven't gone into my appointment yet, but I think I might want to take Cadence to lunch after. Just the two of us. Is that okay? Are you okay with the babies?" she asked.

Tatum faltered at first. Rip was going to take some of his men to work on the HVAC system at the farm, and she really wanted to tag along. She'd charged up her laptop and had the internet wired the day before. It was time to get some clerical work done at the rescue. And if she wanted to be fully operational by the time Christmas rolled around—what with its unwanted gifts and given-up puppies and kittens—then she *really* needed to get going. Particularly with the holidays just weeks away. There was so much to do.

Darla must have understood her hesitation, because she said, "You know what, it's okay. The boys probably need me. I miss them, anyway. I'll be straight home after the appointment and—"

"No, no." Tatum found she had little control over the words spilling from her mouth. "You two go to lunch. You need it. Cadence especially needs it. Talk to her about Christmas, because I'd like to have an idea of what to expect, anyway. When I'll need to have someone stationed at the farm and where we'll be at that time."

There was a pause at the other end of the line before Darla came back on. "Who am I talking to and what have you done with my baby sister?"

Tatum didn't laugh.

"There's a catch, isn't there?" Darla asked.

"No, no. Not a catch, but...you know what, never mind. No catch. Go. Have fun. Talk to Cadence. Get our Christmas plans set. I'll see you when you get home."

AFTER GETTING off the phone with Darla, Tatum shot off a message to Rip. *Any chance you could head to the property without me? I've got the boys until this afternoon.*

He wrote back right away, agreeing to take his crew over and get started without her.

In the meantime, Tatum situated the boys for a midmorning nap and opened her laptop, where she started a document to plan out all things related to opening the shelter. Her notes contained mainly questions, though.

POLICIES AND PROTOCOLS

—Also, regulations and laws (see to-do list)
Dog run and indoor kennels (convert barn?)
Cat house (barn or inside main house?)
Maintain living quarters or convert to offices?
Grand opening date and event, if any
NAME

FOR WHATEVER REASON, naming the place felt like the most important thing, and it should've been the easiest. But Tatum was stuck. Heirloom Island Animal Rescue or Heirloom Island Animal Shelter just didn't *call* to her. She wanted her place on the southern tip of the island to be more than that. She wanted it to be a little haven. That wasn't a bad idea. Heirloom Island Animal Haven?

It still didn't stick. She set the list aside and brought up her working social media accounts. For now, she'd just named those *The Shelter*, which was sort of a hipster thing to do. Tatum was no hipster, but the name wasn't permanent, and the pages weren't live yet. They were in the draft phase, while she created pretty images and well-worded descriptions. The veterinarian she'd consulted had explained to her the basic functions of a shelter, and she even had printouts of the bylaws, regulations, and policies of other county-based shelters. It was a lot of legalese and confusing information, but Tatum had made her way through it, arriving at some simple rules to get started.

Now, she went down the list of her to-dos under that particular category. *County Health Inspection*.

Ugh. Sounded like pure torture. Plus, she wasn't even sure it was time yet for that. Rip was working on the property today. He hadn't yet finished the wall repair in the kitchen (but was close).

Still, she found the phone number and dialed, planning to schedule them for a time in the nearish future.

"County health inspector's office, how can I help you?"

"Hi," Tatum said brightly into the phone. "I'm opening an animal shelter out on Heirloom Island, and I need to book someone to come out for a preliminary inspection for the proper license type?"

The woman's voice came back flat and lifeless, but competent. "Expected opening date?"

"Expected opening date? Oh, um…" Tatum panicked. The right answer was that there *was* no expected opening date. That's what she *should* say. She definitely should not *lie*. She shouldn't fib. She should be truthful. But Tatum's fingers flipped in her mind ahead to two weeks. A Friday. Two weeks should be plenty of time to finish everything up and Friday felt like the appropriate day for a big opening bash. "Exactly two weeks from today," she said airily and with every bit of the confidence of a businesswoman who knew exactly what she was doing.

And exactly when she was doing it.

Even though it absolutely did not occur to her, in that moment, what exactly was two weeks away.

And the woman, efficient and competent and impatient as she was, confirmed. "Two weeks from today. In which case, we'd need to make our initial assessment today. Are you available between ten and noon? We have an auditor on the island for a different project this morning. They can come after, if that works for you?"

Tatum, seized by excitement and forward motion and all things that she wasn't really used to feeling, nodded enthusiastically as she regained the voice that cracked. "Yes. *Yes*. I'll be there."

CHAPTER 28—CADENCE

Cadence arrived at the lakefront office of Dr. Kirk Sanders. His house was a quaint white walk-up with an old-fashioned wood doctor's sign hanging out front. Discreetly displaying *Dr. Kirk Sanders*. Nothing about his being a psychiatrist or psychologist or therapist. A mental doctor.

Cadence appreciated this.

She rang the bell and waited for a secretary—maybe his wife, even?—to answer, but instead, the door swung open to a tall, tan-skinned, dark-haired man of about forty-five or so. He wore wire-rimmed glasses, but they did little to age him, Cadence thought.

"You must be Cadence," he greeted coolly.

She stumbled to reply, as though she'd forgotten her own name. Something about him struck her as remarkable. Perhaps it was the fact that she'd never met him, despite knowing the majority of islanders. Perhaps it was the fact that he was a therapist, and Cadence wasn't sure she'd ever actually met a therapist in person before. In her small world, therapy was reserved for the very rich...or the very, well, *broken*.

Cadence wasn't very rich—not anymore. Did that mean she was—? She couldn't think about that right now. "Yes. I'm Cadence. Cadence Van Dam," she added proudly. She knew the weight of her last name, but as she delivered it, he didn't react. Not how she expected.

"I'm Dr. Sanders." He was austere in his self-introduction, nothing like what she'd hoped for in a small-island doctor who operated out of his little white clapboard lakefront house. But his face wasn't severe to match his words, and he stepped aside, inviting her into a cozy parlor with two blue armchairs, an olive-green loveseat, and a whitewashed coffee table. Missing from both Dr. Sanders and his quaint office room were all the dark woods and heavy, leather-bound hardback collections that a male doctor evoked in her mind.

Instead, the effect of his decor and his own style was comfortable and casual and...hopeful?

"May I?" He indicated her coat, and she slid it off and into his hands. He hung it on a standing coatrack near the door and led her away from the hall and into the parlor proper.

She let out the breath she'd been holding and said, "Thank you."

"Take a seat," he said, gesturing vaguely to the three available options. She assumed he'd take an armchair, as it'd be strange if he didn't. So, Cadence herself lowered to the loveseat, sinking into its pliable cushions, feeling warm after stepping in from the cold, soggy day outside. That day was shaping up to be warmer than usual, and the snow was threatening to melt by the afternoon, which gave the air a heavy moisture to it. But soon enough, winter chill would return in full force with the revival of a cold front the following week. She unwound her scarf, too, rolling it around her hand like a boxer wrapping up before the big fight.

Dr. Sanders dropped into the closer of the two armchairs, and Cadence took in his outfit. He dressed a bit like a woodsman, in a red flannel shirt, jeans, and heavy brown hiking boots. His glasses, Cadence realized, were the only part of him that indicated *medical professional*.

"All right, Cadence. Tell me a little about what brings you here today." He leaned back in his chair and pulled a Moleskine notebook from the table nearest him.

Cadence hesitated. Whatever she said, would he write it down? Like a miserable record of her sadness? Or whatever it was the doctors thought was wrong with her?

She licked her lips and studied the scarf wound around her hand. It was easy to recount what had happened before and at the hospital. Maybe the rest could just come with time.

"Well, I had a panic attack earlier this week. It was so *real*, though." So far, this was easier than she thought it would be.

Dr. Sanders nodded, keeping his eyes on her, soft and inquiring but not questioning or accusing.

She waited a beat for him to answer her, even though she hadn't exactly asked a question. When he said nothing, she went on. "It felt physical," she said, now focusing her own gaze out the window, where a red bird flitted across her view and out to the water. She thought the bird must be freezing. But then, if it was so cold, how could it possibly fly? "The ER doctor thought I must have severe anxiety. Maybe depression." She fell silent again, and the bird flew out of view.

"Do you think that's true?" he asked simply.

Cadence realized now that she'd figured it must be. If a doctor said something, it must be true. She'd simply accepted this as the truth. She hadn't questioned it. "I suppose so."

"Why is that?"

"I'm—" Cadence stopped, her mouth parted, leaving open what it was she might say next. What exactly was Cadence? And what was she willing to tell this stranger?

He must have read her reticence, because he tossed the Moleskine back onto the table, crossed one leg over the other, and clasped his hands around his knee. "Why don't we take a step back?"

Oh no. She'd already said too much. She was already too challenging a patient for him, and she'd only just begun. "I'm sorry," she murmured, twisting the scarf tighter and staring at it in embarrassment.

He shook his head and leaned forward. "No, no. I

apologize. I usually like to start with more of an icebreaker. I don't know what's wrong with me today." He smiled, and Cadence suddenly felt a whole lot better. "Let's start over, okay?" She nodded. "I'm Dr. Sanders. You can call me Kirk."

CHAPTER 29—DARLA

Darla was surprised when Cadence replied right after her appointment, agreeing to meet at the Koken for a light lunch.

They arrived at the same time, Darla coming up from the marina and Cadence coming down the boardwalk from the east. They were each bundled up to the nose in their winter layers, and shedding coats and scarves and hats before taking their seats proved to be something of a prelude to their meal. And a surprisingly nice meal, at that. Darla eased into conversation with small talk, bringing Cadence up to speed on how her appointment went—well—and how the babies were doing when she left—fine.

In turn, Cadence revealed that her therapist

seemed nice, and she looked forward to her next appointment, scheduled for after the holidays.

Darla desperately wanted to question this—why wasn't Cadence going sooner and more regularly? But Cadence ended up explaining without prompting. "He's out of town for the rest of the month and won't be back until after the first. Family stuff."

"Oh," Darla replied then took a spoonful of her clam chowder. Nothing beat the Koken's clam chowder on a cold day, and Darla felt—even if it might be fleeting—that life was perfect just then. Especially since there seemed to be a truce burning between her and Cadence. "Kind of like with us."

"What do you mean?" Cadence sipped from her apple cider, its cinnamon stick poking her in the cheek as she did.

"We've got family stuff going on over the holidays, too. That's what it seems like, at least?"

Cadence shrank back, guilt coloring her cheeks. "I overreacted. I was...being a brat."

"A nearly forty-year-old brat. Impressive. Anyway, brat or not, you're obviously still mad at me, and I don't blame you. I was a little frank." Darla looked down at her soup. "Sorry about that."

"Yeah, but you were right." Cadence met her gaze.

"Uh-oh. Is your therapist into self-flagellation or something?"

At that, Cadence laughed. "Not at all. We didn't even really talk about...what you'd expect."

"Then what'd you talk about?"

"Life? I think. It was mainly a get-to-know-you thing."

"Like a first date." Darla said it off-handedly, but Cadence's face turned plum red.

"No. No. Just—like a first appointment." She swirled her cinnamon stick in her drink. "But back to the holidays. I was being dramatic before. Of course the girls will want to come home for the holidays. We'll figure out sleeping arrangements. We've got the living room sofas and the office pullout. My bed is huge. Tatum's, too. It'll be fine. And Lotte is crazy busy. There's a chance she won't make it up here, anyway. She might have a gig."

"A gig? That's exciting." Darla returned to her soup, sprinkling the last of her crackers into it and savoring the final spoonfuls. "So, just something small, then? At our place?"

"Sure. Just us. Maybe invite Rip, since he's family." Cadence slid her gaze away.

"And since he and Tatum are getting close fast. He's over there helping her again today, you know."

"Ugh. I know." Cadence shook her head. "Rip is about the last person I'd set Tatum up with. And anyway, she's so anti-dating, right? Or anti-romance?"

"Well, be that as it may, they seem to be becoming fast friends."

"Friendship is fine. If it goes further, I'll have to say something." Cadence pursed her lips and looked at Darla as if she were expecting a quick agreement.

But Darla's phone was buzzing in her handbag, so she set Cadence's overprotectiveness aside to answer the call. Just as she hit Accept, the line went dead. "Oh, no," she lamented. "I missed her." She gave it a moment for a voice mail to come through but none did. Then, Darla tried calling her back. She waited through a series of rings, and with each one, her stomach clenched and twisted tighter. When it went to Tatum's voice mail, she hung up and looked at Cadence. "She's not answering. Do you think there's an emergency?"

"Of course not," Cadence answered, but the panic in her expression was more pronounced than it had been the day she'd had a full-blown panic *attack*.

Darla forced herself to breathe and redialed

Tatum. Still no answer. She left a voice mail, then sent a text. *Urgent. Call me back. Everything okay???*

"Will you call her, too? Maybe she's avoiding me. Maybe something happened and she's scared to answer my calls."

Cadence looked only barely skeptical as she tried calling on her phone. No answer.

"Try Rip?" Cadence suggested.

"What's his number?" Darla was dialing and redialing Tatum over and over again as she dug in her purse for cash for the bill. "Can you call him?"

Cadence tapped on her phone while standing from the table and assuring Darla that it was fine. Everything was going to be fine. Tatum and the boys were *just fine*.

CHAPTER 30—TATUM

Tatum tried to call Darla before getting the boys into their car seats in the car and on the road. But Darla didn't answer.

Figuring she had enough lead time to get to the farmhouse and then drive inland for service in order to text or call Darla then, she quickly became distracted with all the things the twins would require for a brief trip to the southern coast. Without good heat, they'd need their winter getups in addition to blankets. She'd better bring the pack 'n play in case they were there more than an hour. Darla had milk stored in both the fridge and the freezer, but Tatum was confused about what to use when and how much, so she found a cooler, packed it with ice, and slotted ten six-ounce bottles in there. Several changes of clothes and a pack of diapers ought to tide them over, she figured, and by the time she was on the road, she realized she'd set her phone down somewhere in the house and left it behind.

But that was okay, because Rip would be at the farmhouse, and Tatum could just send a message from his phone. Anyway, Darla mustn't be too concerned if she didn't have her phone on her and at the ready. So it was fine, Tatum reasoned. It'd all be fine. Darla would understand it was an emergency. Cadence would defend Tatum if Darla didn't understand. And Rip would be there as an objective third party to keep everyone's head cool in times of stress.

That's what Tatum was counting on, at least.

But as she neared the farmhouse, she realized that she was running late. The county health inspector had already arrived—as evidenced by a white truck with patches of snow partially covering the county website and phone number emblazoned on the side.

"Okay, you two," she directed the boys. "We have to be on our best behavior." After finally figuring out how to unfold and lock open the stroller, she scrambled the boys out of their seats before realizing that, to go in the double stroller, the car seats had to go with them. Back into their car seats the boys went.

Then, juggling them awkwardly into the two-seater, only to learn that strollers were more like wheelchairs than four-wheel-drive trucks, she just barely pushed her way through the snow.

Fortunately, Rip must have seen out the window that she was struggling because just in the nick of time before the boys' little red noses turned white with frostbite, he rushed out, scooped the double-wide stroller up in one quick lift, and brought them all inside, closing the door behind them.

Warmth settled over Tatum and the boys. Gabriel started to fuss, though, and Tatum started to freak out. "The health inspector is here for a preliminary walk-through. Can you...help?"

"Oh, it's already underway. I walked him through the HVAC system—where we're at with that. I showed him the wall in the kitchen—it's finished by the way. I stayed late last night after all." He winked at her, and Tatum's insides were in danger of becoming mush.

"You didn't have to do that," she scolded, scooping up Baby Gabriel and pressing a bottle to his lips. He drank greedily, but Shepard started crying, too. Without Tatum asking him to do so, Rip picked up the second baby and reached for a second bottle.

"I had nieces, remember," he said, but his eyes glazed over as he watched the baby feed.

"Right." Tatum glanced around the place. "So, is he still here? The inspector? I mean, I saw the truck out front."

"I'm here, all right!" a voice boomed from the kitchen. Tatum looked to see a burly, bearded man with a clipboard in one hand and a kitten in the other. "Rip says these are for sale?"

Tatum looked at Rip, then back at the stranger. "Do you two—"

Rip shrugged with Baby Shepard still sucking his bottle in his arms. "We work together on some of my other projects."

Tatum liked the way Rip spoke. She liked how he referred to the shelter as though it was one of his projects and everything else was *other*. In just a couple of days, they'd grown close. It was happening fast, but then...was that wrong? Was it wrong to fall in love with someone so quickly? Or maybe Tatum wasn't falling in love. Maybe she was infatuated with Rip because he was helping her bring her dream to life.

Then again, how could she *not* fall in love with the one person who showed up to bring her dream to life? She let the questions rest in her brain for now. "That's Ebenezer," she said of the calico kitten. "He's a little cranky, but I have a feeling he'll come around."

"You've named the kittens?" Rip asked.

"Christmas names."

"Like Miracle," he said, referring to the dog he'd now informally adopted from her.

"Yeah, I guess you and I are sort of on the same level somehow."

"So, is Ebenezer available?" the county health inspector asked.

Tatum returned Gabriel's bottle to the cooler and lifted him to her shoulder, patting his back as if it were the most natural thing in the world. Maybe it was. "Ebenezer? You mean available as in...?" She looked from Rip to the inspector and back again.

Rip shrugged again. "He loves pets, too. Wants a barn cat for his farm on the mainland, I bet. Am I right, Steve?"

"Yup. Just lost our Nan a few months back to pancreatic cancer." He looked a little sullen. "She'd been a stray, and we took her to every shelter from here to Lansing, but no one would take her."

"That's terrible." Tatum clicked her tongue. "It's such a problem, too, stray cats."

"Not for you, though. Seems like you've got a

great place here. I think your project is going to be the highlight of Heirloom Island."

"Really?" Tatum's heart leapt at this morsel of confidence.

"Sure. I can't give you the full license to operate yet. You've got to submit your proposal to Donna first. But I can give you a provisional emergency license. There aren't the same restrictions for animal care facilities as there are for human ones, so this"—he pulled a slip of paper from his clipboard and passed it her way—"will tide you over until all the paperwork is filed."

She took the page without glancing at it. "Really? That's amazing." Her pulse raced, and she patted Gabriel's back in time with it.

"Yep, really. We just need your John Hancock and the business name here. Then I'll sign, too, and I'll take the carbon copy, and you're off to the races."

"Great!" Tatum set Gabriel back into his car seat and set about signing away her life, but it wasn't until she'd added the date that she realized he'd also asked for the business name.

"I don't have a name yet," she admitted, finally reading the page she had just signed.

"Um..." The man fumbled through the pages of his clipboard as if to come up with a remedy. "I suppose you could call our offices on Monday? Maybe come out there and file the name?"

"Can't you do it, Steve? I mean can't we leave it blank for now, and you can add the business name later?"

"Ahh—" Steve made a strange sound, and it occurred to Tatum that this wasn't their usual process. That maybe Rip's friendship had something to do with Steve's easy way, and that maybe even little baby Ebenezer did, too.

She narrowed her eyes at him. "Can you give me five minutes?"

"Five minutes to name the business? Seems like a big ask of you. Lotta pressure, I mean."

"Just five minutes." She looked at him, then at Rip and held up five fingers. "Five minutes." Then she turned to pull her phone from her back pocket. But it wasn't there. And just as she realized that, the front door slammed open.

"Tatum Eugenia Sageberry!" Darla roared as she raced through the door and beelined to Shepard and Gabriel—and therefore, Rip and Steve.

Cadence was hot on her heels, swearing like a sailor at Tatum all the while crying from relief as she grabbed Shepard and Darla scooped up Gabe. "We were worried *sick*. Why weren't you answering your phone?"

"I forgot it at home. I had to come here. I'm so sorry, Darla. I tried to call you—"

"But you didn't respond when I called back? No text? I thought the worst! Tatum! I thought the absolute *worst*. You know that I called the hospital on the mainland before we even came here?"

Cadence added, "And I had 9-1-1 all cued up on my phone."

"Then how did you find us?" Tatum asked, confused and mortified and feeling like the worst version of herself right about then. The version that put animals first. That didn't value family or care about them or think of them above everything else. The version that dominated all her life.

Rip held up his hand weakly. "I was going to tell you they were trying to reach out to you, but—"

"Thank goodness he had the sense to answer his phone. And thank goodness his cell provider covers service the south edge of the island." Cadence hooked a thumb at her brother-in-law, but her resentment dwindled like a melting snowflake on an ember. "I'm just glad you're all okay. All of you." She cupped Tatum's face in her hand, and Tatum felt sick that she had made her sisters feel so sick.

"Darla, I'm so sorry," Tatum whispered. She felt emotion well up behind her eyes and realized that this very moment could be the first time she'd cried since their dad died. It felt too soon. Too raw. "I'm so sorry. If you want to kill me, you totally can. I'll do anything to make this up to you."

Darla, having checked on her boys and settled with them into the rocking chair that had been left in the farmhouse, moved her little family to and fro in slow rocks for a moment before finally looking up at Tatum. "It's okay. It's okay, Tatum. I know you'd never do anything to put them in danger. I just—I panicked."

"We all panic sometimes," Cadence murmured sardonically. "Take it from me."

Tatum smiled at that, and Darla did, too. "So, why did you come here, anyway? What was the emergency?" Darla asked.

"I guess it wasn't technically an emergency," Tatum confessed meekly.

"That's how I felt about my panic attack," Cadence said, this time less sardonically and more softly.

"Sometimes, what is an emergency to one person, may not be to another. The shelter's important to you, Tatum. And I've taken advantage, assuming you can watch the boys for me as if you're my on-call babysitter." Darla frowned. "I'm sorry."

"I should be your on-call babysitter, though," Tatum replied. "That's my job as your sister." She looked down at the babies in her sister's arms. "And you two are my nephews. I'd go to the ends of the earth for you all."

"And today, you went to the end of Heirloom Island," Rip pointed out, unhelpfully.

"Yeah, well, that was for *me*."

Cadence butted in. "But look at all this." She waved a hand about her, indicating the package of diapers, the pack 'n play, the car seats and the stroller, and the cooler of milk that Rip had hauled in. "Maybe the trip was for you, but you didn't sacrifice the boys."

"Cadence is right. We're on this crazy ride together, and that means that each of us has to give somewhere. And I feel like"—Darla let out a heavy sigh—"I feel like everyone has just been giving to *me*." She frowned. "What about *you* two? I've been so selfish."

"No, you've been having babies. That makes you distinctly *not* selfish," Tatum pointed out.

But Darla shook her head. "Still, we have to be here for each other—all of us. Not just for me or even for the boys. Yes, they might be my priority, but that doesn't mean we should give less attention to your dream here, Tatum, or to Cadence's dream, either."

"What's Cadence's dream?" Rip asked innocently.

Cadence shook her head and smiled toward Heaven. "At this point? I think my only dream at this point is to have a successful Christmas."

"What about your events business?" Darla asked. "That was a dream."

"And going back to teaching. Once upon a time, that was your dream," Tatum pointed out.

"Sure, but...it's a lot. I think that can wait. All of it. For the future. Don't you?"

"Why?" Darla asked. "Why not go for it now?"

"Well, for starters, I might not be able to go back to teaching. We'll just have to see what the future holds. If Darla wants to go back to work, one of us has to be home with the babies."

"Unless we find a babysitter," Darla pointed out. "A full-time babysitter, too. Not Tatum and Angus and the rest of her motley crew."

The others laughed, but Tatum turned earnest. "I could be a full-time babysitter."

"No, you have *this*," Darla answered.

"I could do both. Hanging out with animals all day doesn't take a whole lot of attention. Just my mere presence, really. Some phone call answering, maybe."

"Okay, let's just say that Tatum really wants to babysit the boys—and she can manage it—that still leaves the fact that I have no event to plan. So, like I said. Can we set my dreams off for the time being? Focus on you two for now? That's my *biggest* dream, actually. That you two are happy and healthy. Well"—she looked at the boys—"you *four*."

"I know of an event that might need planning," Steve the health inspector inserted.

Everyone turned to him, a stranger in their midst. Goofy and still cuddling Ebenezer Kitten up to his chest, Steve was wholly out of place, and yet, every last one of them was dying to hear what he had to say.

"What?" Tatum asked at last.

He referred to his clipboard. "The grand opening for Heirloom Island's first ever animal rescue."

"Oh!" Darla beamed. "That's true!" She looked at Tatum. "What are you going to name it? Are you going to name it Heirloom Island Animal Rescue?"

"I thought you liked The Haven. Or was it The Shelter?" Cadence asked.

Tatum thought for a moment. "No. I think it's got to have an important name. A name that does refer to rescue or shelter, yes. But something maybe..."

"Biblical?" Cadence offered. "Sorry, sometimes Mom just speaks through me. I can't help it."

Darla laughed, but Rip held up a finger. "What about The Island Igloo?"

Tatum looked at him in bewilderment. "I like you, Rip, but *no*."

"Your opening is so close to Christmas, what if you go with The Nativity? It means the birth of your shelter." Darla looked proud of her suggestion. "And it's got that somber thing going for it, too."

"Well, when *is* the opening?" Cadence asked. "If it's after the New Year, we might want to stick to something more perennial, right?"

Again, Steve spoke up, referring to his clipboard and announcing the date with as much pageantry as one might expect from a county health inspector. "Two weeks from today. Which puts us at..."

Rip did the math in his head faster than anyone else. "December 24."

"December 24?" Cadence shrieked. "Tatum, that's Christmas Eve!"

Tatum's eyes grew wide. "Oh, no."

"Oh, yes," Darla answered, amused by Tatum's latest foible. Her latest blunder.

Tatum buried her face in her hands. "Oh, no no no." She jerked her head up and looked at Steve. "Can we change the date? Please?"

"Well—" he started, but Cadence held up her hand.

"Wait a minute."

"What?" Tatum asked miserably.

"I think it's a fabulous idea. We have it on Christmas Eve." Cadence stepped backward, holding her hands out in inspiration. "Here. At the little farmhouse with the barn out back. A beautiful, snow-draped setting the day before Christmas. It's perfect."

"It is?" Tatum asked.

"Yes," Cadence confirmed. "It is."

At that moment, and in perfect synchronization, the twins started fussing in Darla's arms. "Oh, I just fed them," Tatum pointed out worriedly. "What's wrong now?" She wanted to know what to do in these circumstances. If she was going to babysit, she needed the tricks of the trade.

Darla shushed the babies and rocked them. "Sometimes they just fuss. Diaper change?"

"Check."

"Burped?"

"Check."

"They might be tired. We could tuck them into their car seats. They sometimes like to sleep in them. It's cozy."

"Or maybe they need to be swaddled?" Tatum asked, having read up on the subject earlier that morning when she had a little downtime.

"Just like..." Cadence's eyes were wild and dreamy. "Just like the story of Christmas. 'And this will be a sign for you. You will find a baby wrapped in swaddling clothes and lying in a manger.'"

Tatum's eyes lit up, and her heart thumped fast. She looked first at Rip, who was grinning like a fool. Then at Steve, who nuzzled his new little baby kitten. Then at Darla and Cadence, and finally, at her two sweet nephews, those special boys who'd rocked her world. "It's perfect," she said. "We'll call it The Manger House."

EPILOGUE

It was a huge risk, hosting a grand opening event on Christmas Eve. But the Sageberry sisters were nothing if not risk-takers. This had become all too clear.

To the party, Tatum opted to wear something on-theme *and* functional, in the face of cuddling so many cuties. Relaxed jeans, a pretty red flannel top, and a green scarf, looped around her neck comfortably. It was to be a casual event despite Cadence's admonishments that anything deemed *event* was decidedly not casual. But that was something Cadence would have to learn about Tatum. She marched to the beat of her own Drummer Boy, and if she wanted to wear jeans to the grand opening of her animal rescue, then jeans she would wear.

Rip showed up in similar style: fitted jeans and a worn green sweater on top. Tatum liked the way he looked in jeans. It reminded her, oddly but in a comforting way, of their father. They'd agreed that the event could maybe be like a date, but it turned out nothing had changed between them since that first week he'd offered to help her. They were as comfortable and happy as a pair of high school sweethearts. As comfortable and as happy as a couple who'd been together forever.

After Tatum had done the rounds, making introductions and cutting a big fat red ribbon, Rip stole her away to the lone bedroom she'd kept for overnights at The Manger House. Once inside, he got a little awkward, and this made Tatum giggly and awkward, too. Eventually, he grabbed both her hands and gave his arms a shake and his head a shake and then even shook his legs out. "Tatum," he started, nervous as an elf on Christmas Eve, "I'm not sure what you're looking for." He blinked and seemed to inwardly curse himself. "Heck, I'm not sure what I'm looking for. But, I guess, what I mean to say is, well, actually, it's not something I mean to say, it's something I mean to do."

With that, he pulled out a sprig of mistletoe, a

miniature green bough tied off in a slim, lace ribbon. "Can I—?"

Tatum didn't wait. She moved her hands from his and gripped his broad shoulders, pulling herself to his level and closing her eyes. His lips met hers in a chaste brush, and it sent chills up her spine. She wanted more of this. Much, *much* more. Tatum wanted to kiss Rip. And she wanted to hold him. She wanted to love him.

Maybe, one day, she'd want to marry him.

But for now? A kiss above the mistletoe, the little green spur he held in his hand, would do.

When they parted, their eyes dreamy and dazed and their lips hungry for more, Tatum couldn't help it. She couldn't wait. A kiss alone, perhaps, wouldn't do. "What comes next?" she whispered to him urgently. Feverishly.

"What do you mean?" he asked in return.

"Do we go back out there? Do we *tell* people?"

Rip laughed. "Tell people that we kissed? If you want to, I guess."

"For now, how about this?" She slipped her hand into his and tugged him to the door.

He grinned as they strode out, then murmured to her, "I guess it's true what they say."

"What's that?" she asked, smiling up at him.

"Good things come to those who...what's the saying?"

Tatum smirked. "Rush in."

NEAR THE FIREPLACE, Darla stood with the boys strapped to her chest. They were beginning to gain weight and feel heavier on her. Like a turn in the seasons, she was beginning to see that, after Christmas, things might change. She might go back to teaching. Or, if Tatum was earnest, things might *not* change. Darla might want more time away from them. Or, she might not. She lifted a cup of cider to her lips, nursing it. Relishing it. Little moments like these, the quiet of her babies and the good taste of a party drink, carried a little more meaning than they ever had before. The fire popped near her, and she moved away, weaving through the crowd to the kitchen, to see what food there might be to graze on. The offerings were perfect. Cadence had made sure of that. Veggie platters and stuffing, miniature turkey sandwiches on decadent croissants. Along with the classic cider, she'd made wassail, hot cocoa, and spiced rum. For desserts, a whole table spread across the back wall. Apple and pumpkin pies; pecan and gooseberry, too. Darla smiled at the gooseberry. It was something their mother had made every Christmas when they were girls. Gooseberries were hard to come by, which added a specialness to the tart treat. She cut herself a slice and plated it, turning to find a sister or one of the Van Dam girls, maybe.

Instead, though, a different figure appeared in the door.

"We *have* to stop meeting like this," she said to Mason in a low, cloying voice. It'd become a joke since he seemed to have become their right-hand man.

He laughed, but his eyes twinkled with something other than humor. Hope? She wished. "With Rip and Tatum on the fast track of love, I'm afraid you're not likely to shake me. He's my best friend."

"Your best friend?" she teased. "I thought *I* was your best friend."

He slipped a hand into one pocket and swaggered nearer, plucking a plastic fork from the table and plunging it into her dessert. "Nope," he answered, popping the forkful into his mouth and chewing. She watched the muscles in his jaws work and wished with every fiber of her being that she'd never said what she'd said before. She hadn't meant it. But then, hadn't she? If Darla was anything, she was a good woman. A decent one. And now, she was a mother. She simply couldn't date.

At least, not *yet*.

"If I'm not your best friend," she said back, taking his fork and using it to scoop her own piece into her mouth, "then what am I?"

Mason took a napkin and wiped his mouth, then kissed his fingertips and patted the backs of each of her babies.

"Hopefully," he said, unsmiling, his lips almost shaky, "you're my future."

CADENCE WAS PLEASED with the event. She'd pulled off quite the Christmas miracle, carting in fresh wreaths and twinkling white lights, little stuffed Santas, and even a beautifully carved wooden Nativity, which she'd displayed on the hearth in the parlor. She remained most proud of the tree, however. At home, it had simply felt too hard to pull out and put up the Christmas tree that she and Hendrik had always decked together. It felt, actually, impossible. But here at Tatum's Manger House? Anything felt possible. Even confronting the past.

And maybe...confronting the future. As she twisted an errant ornament on one of the front boughs of the grand-sized artificial Douglas fir, a familiar voice intoned her name from behind. "Cadence?"

She swiveled around, initially unable to place the voice or the man. But it came as perfectly as snow on Christmas Day. "Dr. Sanders."

"Kirk," he corrected.

She flashed a smile, gesturing about with her mulled wine. "What brings you here? Weren't you supposed to be out of town?"

He tucked his free hand into his pocket and glanced down, then back up. "My family plans changed at the last minute. So here I am." He gave her a winning smile. "Plus, I'm sponsoring the dog run for Ms. Sageberry. She's your sister, I gather?"

"Yes. My baby sister. And thank you," Cadence said.

Silence filled the night air between them, and the fire crackled behind her. She ran her tongue over her teeth, thinking of the next right thing to say. It didn't come, and so she simply smiled at him.

"How long have you lived here?"

"On the island?" she asked.

He nodded her on, swigging from his drink—a

spiced rum by the looks of it. She wondered if he liked it. If he liked her recipe. Her decorations. Her *event*.

Instead of wondering all that aloud, however, she simply answered his question. "Since I left college and got my first teaching job here, at St. Mary's Catholic School."

"That's right, the little schoolhouse next to the church."

"Are you Catholic?" The question fell from her mouth, and she wanted to reel it back in. It was wildly inappropriate for her to ask her therapist for his religion.

But to her surprise, he gave a short nod. "Confirmed and everything. Haven't practiced in years, though. Maybe since before you moved here. That makes me a casual Catholic, I guess."

"To each his own," she remarked.

He held up his drink. "I like that. To each his *or her* own."

They clinked glasses, and Cadence swept the room with her eyes again, looking for abandoned plates, wandering guests, that sort of thing.

When it occurred to her that Kirk had settled there, by her side, she figured she ought to continue the polite small talk. "How about you?"

"How long have I lived here?"

She nodded.

"Just six months. I moved over this summer."

She couldn't help it; a nagging question made its way up. "What brought you here to Heirloom? Family?" she guessed.

He shook his head. "If I had to put a finger on it, I'd say fresh air." A wide grin pushed his cheeks back and revealed perfect teeth. A symmetrical face. Attractive, objectively. Also *irrelevantly*.

"Fresh air? Well, we have plenty of that," she replied.

"Actually, I inherited my mother's business."

Cadence's ears perked up. "She was a therapist?"

He smiled and nodded. "Mhm. And the house was hers. Mine, too, I guess. When I was a kid. Grew up here. Left for college. Got married. All that."

Cadence bit her tongue about the married part. "I see. And now you're back."

"Yep. And I suppose it's sort of becoming a *thing*, as the kids say."

"What do you mean?" Cadence asked.

"Folks moving back to the island. I've met three of my old schoolmates since I got here. They'd all left, too. And came back."

"Ah. It's interesting to hear that our population is

growing, rather than dwindling. Could be good for the school, I suppose." She always connected things back to the school. Island population. Parishioner count. It all mattered for St. Mary's.

Kirk frowned at her. "Do you mean St. Mary's?" he asked.

She laughed at that. "What other school would I be talking about? Birch Harbor already gets all the mainland kids."

"You know, the new one. That's going up this winter?"

"New one? What are you talking about?" Cadence asked scornfully.

"There's a new charter school. One of the guys I graduated with is a school administrator, and he's bringing a whole new charter school to the island. Building on the east coast, almost right on the water." He took a drink, then something dawned on him. She saw this in his face. Maybe in the same way something was dawning on her. A bitter realization.

"Oh no," he murmured. "I'm sorry. I figured you knew since you're a teacher here. And Rip—Rip Van Dam. He's a friend of yours. In-law, I take it?"

"You know the Van Dams?"

"Went to school with them." He said this all so simply. So casually. Like it didn't matter. Like the fact that he'd known Hendrik didn't matter. And like the fact that a new school going up on the island *didn't matter.*

In that moment, Cadence knew something for certain. And lately, she hadn't known much for certain. She hadn't known if she had anxiety or depression or PTSD. She hadn't known if she'd ever get over Hendrik's passing. She hadn't known if it would work with this therapist. Especially now, hearing that there could be a conflict of interest—they ran in the same circles, in a way.

But what she knew right then and right there was that she would be returning to St. Mary's. As soon as Christmas was over and the New Year passed and the twelve days had come and gone and resolutions were made and broken. She'd return.

And maybe, she'd even make an event of it.

THANK you for reading *The Manger House*. Continue the series with Cadence's story in *The Abbey House*.

ALSO BY ELIZABETH BROMKE

Heirloom Island:

The Boardwalk House (1)

The Manger House (2)

The Abbey House (3)

Other Series

Prairie Creek

Harbor Hills

Birch Harbor

Hickory Grove

Gull's Landing

Maplewood

ACKNOWLEDGMENTS

I'd like to give a special thanks to Elise Griffin, Beth Attwood, and Tandy O. of Eagle Eye Proofreading. Thank you fabulous ladies for helping my stories shine! I couldn't do it without you!

As always, a big thank-you to my close friends and family for unending patience and support. I love each and every last one of you.

To my incredible ARC readers, fans, and bookworm friends, I can only write books and enjoy my dream career because of YOU. THANK YOU!

Ed, Eddie, Winnie, and Tuesday—all for you!

ABOUT THE AUTHOR

Elizabeth Bromke writes women's fiction and contemporary romance. She lives in the mountains of northern Arizona with her husband, son, and their sweet dogs, Winnie and Tuesday.

Learn more about the author by visiting her website at elizabethbromke.com.

Made in the USA
Columbia, SC
23 November 2021